THE BRIDE

AN UNTAMED HEARTS OF THE WEST BOOK

by Samuel DenHartog

Copyright © 2025 by Samuel DenHartog.
All rights reserved.

No part of this publication may be reproduced, distributed, or transmitted in any form or by any means, including photocopying, recording, or other electronic or mechanical methods, without the prior written permission of the publisher, except as permitted by U.S. copyright law.

The story, all names, characters, and incidents portrayed in this production are fictitious. No identification with actual persons (living or deceased), places, buildings, and products are intended or should be inferred.

Published by STUDIOS SINALOA

1st Edition. 2025.

Table of Contents

[CHAPTER 1] — DAUGHTER OF TWO WORLDS.....................3

[CHAPTER 2] — THE HEALER'S TOUCH................................18

[CHAPTER 3] — THE LONE MUSTANG..................................29

[CHAPTER 4] — A PLACE AT THE FIRE 40

[CHAPTER 5] — SHADOWS ON THE HORIZON....................54

[CHAPTER 6] — BLOOD AND ASHES 63

[CHAPTER 7] — A STRANGER AMONG THEM 70

[CHAPTER 8] — THE EDGE OF DEATH..................................81

[CHAPTER 9] — BETWEEN HOSTILITY AND HEALING.........95

[CHAPTER 10] — THE GREAT DIVIDE 104

[CHAPTER 11] — THE TIES THAT BIND 116

[CHAPTER 12] — BENEATH THE PAINTED SKY 126

[CHAPTER 13] — TREADING DANGEROUS GROUND........137

[CHAPTER 14] — THE FIRST KISS 147

[CHAPTER 15] — THE WEIGHT OF DESIRE 155

[CHAPTER 16] — THE SOLDIERS DRAW NEAR 162

[CHAPTER 17] — BETWEEN LOVE AND LOYALTY..............170

[CHAPTER 18] — THE REGIMENT ARRIVES 178

[CHAPTER 19] — A CHOICE OF THE HEART.......................184

[CHAPTER 20] — THE COMANCHE BRIDE..........................193

[CHAPTER 21] — A STRANGER IN A NEW LAND................205

[CHAPTER 22] — THE COST OF LOVE 213

[CHAPTER 23] — A FIRE THAT WILL NEVER DIE 221

ABOUT THE AUTHOR 225

[CHAPTER 1] — DAUGHTER OF TWO WORLDS

Tala Sky pressed her heels lightly against her mare's sides, urging the horse into a smooth, effortless gallop across the rolling plains. The wind swept her dark hair back, sending it trailing behind her like a banner, and she let out a slow breath, savoring the feeling of it against her face. The scent of dry grass and distant rain filled her lungs, and for a moment, there was nothing but the rhythm of the hooves beneath her, the pulse of the land beneath them, and the vast sky stretching overhead. Here, under the open heavens, she belonged to no one but herself.

In the distance, the earth trembled with the pounding of hooves—wild mustangs, running free. Tala slowed her mare and turned toward the movement, shading her eyes against the sun. A herd of at least two dozen moved like a living tide, their sleek bodies gleaming in the late afternoon light. The lead stallion, a powerful black with a white blaze down his face, surged ahead, his strides long and full of unbroken spirit. Behind him, mares and foals followed, kicking up dust as they thundered across the land. They were untamed, untouched by the hands of men, and watching them sent a shiver down her spine.

The sight stirred something deep inside her, something restless and wild. She had been raised among the Comanche, but she would never be fully one of them. The blood of a white man coursed through her veins, an inheritance she had

[CHAPTER 1] — DAUGHTER OF TWO WORLDS

never asked for yet could not escape. Even now, no matter how well she rode, how many medicines she learned, how much she worked to prove herself, there would always be those who saw her as different. And yet, watching the mustangs, she wondered—was she ever meant to belong to one place? Or was she like them, meant to roam free, untethered, beholden to no one?

Her mare shifted beneath her, sensing her rider's hesitation. Tala exhaled, loosening the reins. "Maybe I ain't meant to stay anywhere," she murmured, though there was no one to hear her but the wind. She glanced at the herd again, watching as the stallion reared up and let out a sharp call to his band before they disappeared into the rolling hills. A part of her longed to follow them, to see where they would run next, to leave behind everything that weighed on her shoulders.

Instead, she turned her horse toward the camp.

By the time she reached the outskirts, the sun had dipped lower in the sky, painting everything in hues of amber and rose. Smoke curled from the tipi fires, carrying the scent of roasting meat and herbs. Children darted between the tipis, their laughter rising bright and carefree as they ran barefoot through the dust, playing games of chase. Tala smiled faintly as one little girl shrieked in delight, ducking away from her older brother's outstretched hands.

But not all the gazes upon her were so innocent.

The moment she passed through the camp, she felt the weight of wary eyes upon her. A few men glanced her way and quickly looked elsewhere, unwilling to be caught staring, but the women were not so subtle. Some merely

[CHAPTER 1] — DAUGHTER OF TWO WORLDS

watched her with quiet appraisal, their expressions unreadable. Others, particularly the older ones, let their disapproval show plainly, their lips pressed into thin lines, their gazes cool and measuring. She had seen those looks all her life—the silent reminders that, no matter how long she lived among them, she would never be entirely Comanche.

Tala lifted her chin and kept riding, refusing to let it sink into her bones the way it always tried to. She had earned her place here, even if not everyone agreed. She had tended to the sick, healed the wounded, gathered herbs in the deep woods when no one else dared venture in alone. She had done everything asked of her, yet it would never be enough for some.

Near the center of the camp, a small group of women sat together, their hands busy weaving or mending, their conversation halting as she approached. She recognized most of them—women who had known her mother, women who had whispered about her father. One of them, an older woman with silver strands woven through her braids, narrowed her eyes slightly as Tala passed.

"She spends too much time out there alone," the woman muttered, not bothering to lower her voice. "Riding across the plains like some wild thing, like she ain't got a place here."

Another woman beside her, younger but just as watchful, let out a quiet hum. "Maybe she don't. Maybe that's why she's always runnin' off."

Tala stiffened but did not slow. She had learned long ago not to let them see her falter. If she gave them even a

[CHAPTER 1] — DAUGHTER OF TWO WORLDS

sliver of doubt, they would carve it into her flesh like a blade.

Not all of them felt the same. As she passed by another tipi, an old woman sitting outside lifted her gaze and nodded once in quiet greeting. Tsénatokwa, the camp healer—the one person who had never questioned Tala's place. Her gaze was knowing, steady, as if she saw past the gossip and the sideways glances and recognized something deeper inside her.

Tala dipped her head in return before dismounting, The scent of smoldering wood and crushed sage drifted through the air as Tala led her mare toward the small corral at the edge of the camp. She loosened the bridle, murmuring a few quiet words to the horse before giving its strong neck a final pat. The late afternoon sun cast long streaks of light across the packed earth, the warmth lingering even as the evening breeze began to stir. From the center of the camp, the distant sounds of voices and the steady rhythm of work carried toward her—women pounding maize, the low murmur of men speaking in the council tipi, the occasional burst of laughter from children still at play.

Tala hesitated only a moment before turning toward the medicine tipi. The tipi was older than most in the camp, its walls lined with carefully woven reeds, the air inside always thick with the scent of drying herbs and woodsmoke. She had spent more time within its walls than anywhere else, learning the ways of healing from the only person who had ever truly accepted her without question.

Tsénatokwa sat near the fire pit, her hands deftly sorting through a bundle of dried roots, her sharp eyes lifting as Tala entered. The old healer didn't ask why she had come—there was no need. Tala had been coming to her since childhood, seeking wisdom, knowledge, and the quiet reassurance of the one person who had never treated her as less than whole. Without a word, Tsénatokwa gestured to the mortar and pestle beside her.

Tala knelt beside Tsénatokwa, the scent of crushed sage and bitterroot rising as she ground the herbs with a stone pestle. The old woman's hands, lined with years of work, moved with practiced ease, sorting through the small bundles of dried leaves and roots, plucking out what was needed for the next remedy. Tala had done this countless times, since she was a child barely able to lift the stone mortar. Back then, she had struggled under Tsénatokwa's watchful eye, grinding too fast or too slow, crushing the wrong parts, adding too much water. But now, her hands knew the work as if it had always been part of her.

"Good," Tsénatokwa murmured, watching the consistency of the paste Tala was making. "Not too fine, not too thick. Strong enough to pull out fever, but not so bitter they won't take it." She lifted a small pinch of the mixture and brought it to her tongue, nodding in approval. "You listen better than most."

Tala allowed a small smile, though she kept her focus on her work. "You never gave me much choice."

The old woman let out a dry chuckle. "No, I did not."

They worked in silence for a while, the rhythmic scraping of stone against wood filling the air. The medicine tipi smelled of dried sweetgrass and smoke, mixed with the sharp tang of herbs. Bundles of plants hung from the poles above them, casting long streaks of muted light through the roof where the smoke escaped. The warmth of the fire pit in the center of the tipi made the space comfortable, though the air outside had begun to cool with the turn of the seasons.

Tala reached for a handful of willow bark, breaking it into smaller pieces before adding it to the mixture. "This is for the elder with the aching joints?"

Tsénatokwa nodded. "And for the boy who fell from his pony yesterday. His mother frets too much, but it will help the swelling." She paused, her sharp eyes flicking to Tala. "You should chew some yourself. I see the way you tense your shoulders."

Tala shook her head, pressing her lips together. "I'm fine."

Tsénatokwa scoffed. "Always saying you're fine. You think I don't know what you carry? Healing is more than treating wounds, Tala. It is knowing the people who carry them."

Tala exhaled, lowering her gaze. She had heard Tsénatokwa say it many times before, but today, the words settled heavier in her chest. She didn't just mean the sicknesses or injuries that came with life on the plains. She meant the weight in Tala's heart, the burden she never fully put down.

Before she could answer, the flap of the tipi rustled, and a warrior strode past them. Tala recognized Nāhtöh's strong frame even before she saw his face, the set of his shoulders tense as he moved through the camp. He did not pause, did not glance her way, only walked past as if she were nothing more than the smoke curling from the fire.

[CHAPTER 1] — DAUGHTER OF TWO WORLDS

She kept her head still, but her stomach tightened, the slight as familiar as it was painful. She had long learned not to expect acknowledgment from some of the men in the camp, especially those like Nāhtöh, who saw her father's blood as a stain that could never be washed away. But that did not make it sting any less.

Tsénatokwa sighed, shaking her head. "Fools who don't know the value of a strong heart," she muttered under her breath before glancing at Tala. "Do not let that one weigh on you."

Tala forced her hands to keep moving, pressing down on the herbs with a steadiness she did not quite feel. "It does not matter."

Tsénatokwa snorted. "Of course it does."

Tala said nothing, though her fingers curled slightly around the pestle. Her mother had always assured her that one day, she would be fully accepted. That one day, the stares would fade, the whispers would stop, and she would stand among her people as one of them, not something between.

But Esihabi had been wrong. Or perhaps she had simply hoped too much.

The day her mother died, that fragile comfort shattered like ice beneath a spring thaw. The camp had mourned Esihabi, had spoken of her bravery, her kindness, her skill in healing. But their grief had not extended fully to Tala. Without Esihabi's presence, the looks grew colder, the silences heavier. She had been left standing alone in a world that had always hesitated to claim her.

[CHAPTER 1] — DAUGHTER OF TWO WORLDS

She had been fifteen when Esihabi was taken from her. Fifteen when she knelt beside her mother's still body, hands sticky with blood, waiting for the breath that never came. She had wanted to scream, to rage, to demand answers from the sky itself. But she had done none of those things. She had stayed silent, because she had learned early that grief did not change the world.

Tsénatokwa's voice pulled her back. "She was proud of you."

Tala swallowed against the lump in her throat. "She wanted me to belong."

"She wanted you to be strong. And you are." The old woman's voice softened. "But even the strongest must learn that belonging does not come from others. It comes from knowing who you are."

Tala breathed in deeply through her nose, the scent of crushed herbs grounding her. She wished it were that simple.

She thought of her father, a man whose face had faded with time but whose voice still lingered in her mind. Nathaniel Ward had left when she was eight, old enough to remember the warmth of his embrace and the sound of his laughter, but not old enough to understand why he never returned. Had he truly loved her, or had she been a burden he did not wish to carry? Some said he had been killed on a trading route. Others murmured of betrayal, of debts unpaid, of a life abandoned.

She had spent years wondering what was true. Had he fought to return? Had he thought of her at all? Or had he been relieved to be rid of the ties that bound him to the plains?

[CHAPTER 1] — DAUGHTER OF TWO WORLDS

She had no answers. And that, more than anything, was what burned the deepest.

That night, the camp stirred with an energy that set Tala's nerves on edge. The air carried an unease that had not been there before, a shift in the rhythm of life that sent people moving faster, speaking in hushed, urgent tones. The riders had returned.

Tala stood near the medicine tipi, grinding a bundle of dried yarrow between her fingers, but her attention was elsewhere. At the far end of the camp, a group of dust-covered men dismounted from their ponies, their faces set in grim expressions. The horses were lathered with sweat, their flanks heaving. Whatever news the scouting party had brought back, it was not good.

The murmur of voices swelled as more people took notice. Women peered out from their tipis, hands pausing in their work. A few young boys darted closer, wide-eyed and eager for news, but they were quickly called back by their mothers. Tala shifted her weight, her fingers tightening around the herbs she had forgotten she was holding. She had seen this before.

The scouts did not linger. Without pause, they strode toward the central fire where the men would gather, their expressions dark with purpose. Warriors began moving in that direction, their postures tense. Even those who had been resting or tending to weapons stopped what they were doing, drawn by the unspoken summons. The fire had been burning low, little more than embers, but someone fed it more wood, and the flames licked higher, casting long shapes across the packed earth.

[CHAPTER 1] — DAUGHTER OF TWO WORLDS

Tala exhaled slowly and turned back to her work, though her fingers moved without focus. She had no place in such meetings. It did not matter that she had spent her whole life here, or that she had tended to the wounds of some of these men. They would not welcome her into their councils, and she knew better than to try.

Still, curiosity tugged at her.

She wandered toward the edge of the gathering, stopping where the flickering firelight barely reached. Women did not take part in these decisions, but some stood just outside the circle, listening. A few cast her wary glances as she approached, but they did not send her away.

The voices rose as the men took their places around the fire.

"They come closer each season," one of the warriors growled. "They build where they do not belong. It will not stop unless we stop it."

"They are just settlers," another argued. "They are not soldiers."

"They are men who take what is not theirs."

Tala recognized the speaker by his clipped, biting tone—Nāhtöh. He stood with his arms folded across his chest, his sharp gaze scanning the others as he spoke. His face was set like stone, his voice full of conviction. "If we do nothing, more will come. And they will not stop at our hunting grounds. They will take it all, the way they have taken from others." He paused, then let his next words land like a stone dropped into water. "We must strike first."

[CHAPTER 1] — DAUGHTER OF TWO WORLDS

A murmur swept through the gathering, some nodding in agreement, others shifting uneasily.

"We do not know if they mean to push farther," one of the older men countered. "If we move too soon, we bring war upon ourselves."

Nāhtöh let out a breath through his nose, eyes narrowing. "War has already come. We can either meet it on our terms, or let them decide when it reaches us."

More voices joined in, some full of anger, others laced with hesitation. Tala remained still, listening, though she felt the weight of a few eyes drifting toward her.

She knew why.

To some, she was not just a girl standing at the edge of a council meeting. She was a reminder of what they despised. The blood of a white man ran in her veins, the same kind of man who now built cabins near their hunting lands, who cut trees and fenced fields and claimed the earth as if they had been born from it.

Tala met one of the stares—an older warrior she did not know well. His expression was unreadable, but he did not look away.

Tobáhā finally raised a hand, and the voices quieted. The chief's voice was slow, steady, carrying the weight of experience. "Fighting is easy when you have never seen the cost," he said, his gaze sweeping over the gathered men. "I have seen it. More battles than some of you have years."

Nāhtöh bristled but did not interrupt.

Tobáhā continued. "When we fight, we do not fight alone. We fight with our families at our backs, with our women and children in the path of what comes next. And once the blood is spilled, there is no turning back."

The tension thickened. Some warriors looked to one another, weighing the words. Others remained rigid, unwilling to be swayed.

"They will take our land either way," Nāhtöh said, his voice quieter now but no less firm. "And when they do, will we be the ones kneeling, or the ones standing?"

The fire crackled, sending up small embers into the night air.

Tala's fingers dug into her palms.

No decision was made that night. But she could feel it—the shift in the air, the thickening weight of something coming.

She did not know when, or how, but it was coming.

After the meeting was over, Tala sat cross-legged outside her tipi, the coolness of the earth beneath her a steadying presence as she gazed up at the vast spread of stars above. The night was clear, the kind where the sky stretched on forever, a great endless sea pricked with silver light. She had watched these same stars since she was a child, tracing the same constellations her mother had once pointed out to her, the old stories woven into their names still lingering in her mind. But tonight, the sky felt different. Or maybe she was different.

She pulled her blanket tighter around her shoulders, though the night air was not yet cold enough to warrant it. The wind stirred through the camp, carrying the lingering scent of smoke from the council fire, the distant murmur of

[CHAPTER 1] — DAUGHTER OF TWO WORLDS

low voices still speaking even now. The meeting had ended without resolution, but that did not mean it was truly over. It would linger in the minds of the men, turn over in their thoughts like a stone in a river until it was worn down to something clear.

She closed her eyes and let her head tip back. "What would you say, Ina?" Her voice was barely more than a breath, but she said it anyway. "Would you tell me to wait, to let them decide for me? Or would you tell me to ride far away before it's too late?"

The wind gave no answer, only stirred the loose strands of her hair.

She longed for her mother's voice, the calm steadiness of it, the way it could ground her no matter how uncertain she felt. Esihabi had always known how to turn worries into something smaller, something that could be carried instead of crushed beneath. But Esihabi was gone, and all that was left were memories, frayed at the edges, worn thinner with each passing year.

The sounds of the night filled the silence between her thoughts. Crickets hummed their steady song from the grasses, an owl called from somewhere beyond the camp, and the distant howls of coyotes rose and fell like waves against the quiet. It was familiar, yet tonight, something in it set her on edge. She shifted where she sat, rubbing her arms, trying to shake the feeling pressing at her chest.

She didn't know what it was—only that it felt as though something beyond the horizon was calling her.

It made no sense. She had always felt more at peace under the open sky than within walls, had always felt the pull of the land beneath her feet. But this was different. This was a restless kind of feeling, like the air before a storm, when the heat pressed too thick against the skin and the trees stood too still.

She let out a slow breath, staring hard at the stars. "Where do I belong?" The words slipped out before she could stop them. "If I ain't meant to stay, then where?"

The Comanche had raised her, taught her their ways, given her their tongue. But some would never see her as one of them, no matter how much she gave. And the world beyond their lands was just as unforgiving, full of men who would look at her and see nothing but a savage girl who did not belong there either.

She dug her fingers into the blanket wrapped around her, gripping the fabric as if it might anchor her to something solid.

Maybe she would always be caught between the two. Never quite one, never quite the other.

The thought burned.

The voices near the council fire had gone quiet now, leaving only the crackle of dying embers in their wake. A few men still lingered nearby, speaking in low tones, their words too distant to catch. But she did not need to hear them to know what they spoke of. The settlers. The threat. The decision that had yet to be made.

She let out a breath and pulled herself to her feet. She would find no answers sitting out here.

Inside her tipi, the air was still warm from earlier, the faint scent of dried herbs clinging to the woven walls. She unwrapped the blanket from her shoulders and settled onto her sleeping mat, stretching out and staring up at the roof, where the faintest sliver of moonlight filtered through the opening above.

No matter what the others believed about her, no matter the looks or the words left unsaid, she would keep her head high.

[CHAPTER 2] — THE HEALER'S TOUCH

The morning sun cast a golden glow over the camp, painting the rolling plains in hues of amber and rust. Smoke curled lazily from the tipi fires, carrying the mingled scents of burning sage and roasting meat. The air was cool, still holding the remnants of the night's chill, but the promise of another hot day lay heavy against the horizon. Tala stood outside her tipi, rolling her shoulders and taking in the quiet hum of the camp as it stirred to life.

Women moved between the tipis, some carrying baskets of dried maize, others tending to the morning's meal. Children darted past, their laughter ringing through the air as they chased each other between the tipis, bare feet kicking up dust. A group of men gathered near the central fire, voices low as they spoke of the scouts' return the night before. The tension still lingered, even in the light of day, though no one spoke of it outright.

Tala took a slow breath and turned toward the healer's tipi. She had work to do.

The moment she stepped inside, she caught the scent of dried herbs and woodsmoke mingling with the rich, earthy tang of medicinal pastes. Tsénatokwa was already at work, sorting through bundles of fresh plants gathered in the early dawn. The old woman glanced up but said nothing as Tala moved to help, her hands automatically reaching for the tools of her trade.

[CHAPTER 2] — THE HEALER'S TOUCH

Before she could begin, the entrance rustled, and a figure stepped through. Sawáni.

His gait was uneven, and the moment Tala saw the way he held himself, she knew he was hurt. His arm was drawn in close to his body, his side stiff with the careful movements of a man trying not to aggravate fresh wounds. His dark eyes flicked toward her, sharp and unreadable, before shifting back to Tsénatokwa.

"I was told you were back," he said, his voice edged with pain but steady. "Had a run-in with a bull on the hunt."

Tsénatokwa didn't look up from her work. "Did the bull lose?"

Sawáni let out a dry chuckle. "Not before making sure I knew he wasn't happy about it."

Tala crossed the space between them, already assessing the damage. His arm bore a long, jagged gash, fresh but not deep enough to be dangerous. His side was worse—a tear along his ribs, the skin bruised and raw where the beast's horn had caught him. She gestured for him to sit.

"Let me see," she said, crouching beside him.

For a moment, he hesitated, his jaw tightening. Then, with a slow breath, he lowered himself onto the mat, shifting his weight carefully. Tala reached for the bowl of water nearby, dampened a cloth, and began to clean the wound along his arm. His skin was warm beneath her touch, his muscles tense, but he did not flinch.

"You're lucky," she said. "A few inches lower, and you wouldn't be walking in here on your own."

[CHAPTER 2] — THE HEALER'S TOUCH

Sawáni exhaled through his nose. "Didn't feel much like luck at the time."

She worked quickly, her fingers practiced and sure, pressing strips of fresh bark against the wound before binding it with a strip of clean cloth. She could feel the weight of his gaze on her, though he said nothing. When she moved to tend his side, he let out a sharp breath as her fingers brushed against the bruised skin.

"Hold still," she muttered, reaching for a fresh salve.

He let out a grunt but obeyed, though she could still feel his eyes on her. She knew that look—the quiet study, the measuring. It wasn't distrust, not exactly. But it wasn't trust, either.

When she finished, she sat back on her heels, wiping her hands clean on a cloth. "It'll heal fine," she said. "Just don't go wrestling any more buffalo before it does."

A smirk tugged at the corner of his lips, but it was gone just as quick. "I'll do my best."

He pulled his tunic back over his shoulder, adjusting it carefully over the fresh bindings. He didn't move to stand right away, as if considering his next words. Then, finally, he glanced at her. "Thank you."

There was something in his voice that made her pause. Not reluctance, not quite. But hesitation, as if acknowledging her skill was something he did not entirely want to do. She met his gaze evenly, holding it just long enough for him to know she noticed.

She didn't say anything. She didn't have to.

The moment was broken by a noise from outside—low voices, the soft rustle of movement near the entrance. She caught the sound of women speaking, their words just quiet enough to be missed if she hadn't been listening.

"She is good with healing, there's no denying that."

"She learned from Tsénatokwa, same as any of us."

"Yes, but blood carries wisdom, does it not? And hers—"

Tala pressed her lips together, keeping her focus on wrapping the last of Sawáni's bindings. She knew how these conversations went. Some admired her skill, recognized that she had earned it. Others saw her white father's blood as a flaw, something that could not be undone no matter how many years she spent among them.

She forced herself to breathe evenly, keeping her hands steady as she tied the last knot. She would not let them see it get to her.

Skill was proven in action, not words.

She had learned that long ago.

Tala moved with precision, selecting dried herbs from the woven baskets stacked along the medicine tipi's walls. She crushed a handful of willow bark between her palms, the bitter scent rising as she worked, then reached for the small clay bowl where the bear fat warmed over the fire. The salve needed to be thick enough to seal wounds but not so heavy that it would smother them. She stirred in the herbs, watching as the oil from the crushed plants darkened the mixture.

[CHAPTER 2] — THE HEALER'S TOUCH

Her hands worked automatically, but her mind drifted. It often did when she was preparing medicine—her thoughts slipping between the present and the past like water through her fingers.

She remembered being small, no more than four or five, perched on her father's knee as he ran his calloused fingers over the pages of an old book. His voice had been steady, patient, as he traced the letters with one hand and guided her own small fingers with the other.

"This is an A, see?" Nathaniel Ward had said, tapping the letter. "Like the way the wind cuts through the canyon."

She had frowned at the shape, not understanding how a mark on a page could sound like the wind.

"Words have power, little bird," he had murmured, his blue eyes warm with something she had not yet been old enough to name. "They can build bridges or burn them, depending on how you use 'em."

She had not understood what he meant, not then. She had only known that she liked the way he spoke, the way the strange English words tumbled from his lips and wove around her like something secret, something that belonged to just the two of them.

But words had not saved him.

She ground the herbs harder than necessary, her jaw tightening as the memory turned bitter. He had left when she was still young, his pack heavy with trade goods, his rifle slung across his back. It had been a journey like any other, one he had made before, moving between settlements and Comanche camps, always returning with stories and trinkets and laughter in his eyes. Only that time, he had never come back.

Tala told herself it did not matter. He had been gone for more years than he had been present in her life, and yet sometimes, when she least expected it, the loss curled inside her like a wound that had never fully closed.

The small scrape of a wooden staff against the packed earth pulled her back to the present.

Tsénatokwa was watching her. The old woman's sharp gaze missed nothing, though her voice was soft when she finally spoke. "You cannot heal others if you are still wounded yourself."

Tala stiffened, her fingers pausing over the salve. "I ain't wounded."

Tsénatokwa did not argue, only let the silence stretch between them. It was worse than words, that silence. Tala swallowed against the tightness in her throat, turning back to the mixture, forcing herself to focus.

She was not waiting for a ghost.

She was not.

Later that afternoon, Tala walked beside Tsénatokwa as they moved through the thick grass beyond the camp, their steps quiet against the damp earth. The morning had warmed, and the air was rich with the scent of pine and wild sage, the breeze carrying the distant calls of birds hidden among the trees. The old healer walked with purpose, her staff barely stirring the grasses as she led the way toward a small clearing where the best plants grew in the rich soil near the creek. Tala had made this trip countless times since childhood, learning where to find the herbs that eased pain, the roots that drew out fever, and the berries that, if used wrong, could kill a man before nightfall.

She had first followed Tsénatokwa into the forest when she was barely old enough to carry her own basket, her legs struggling to keep up with the old woman's steady pace. Now, her feet knew the way without thinking, each bend in the path familiar, every tree like an old friend.

Tsénatokwa stopped near a patch of low-growing plants, their delicate yellow flowers brushing against the ground. She pointed with the end of her staff. "Tell me."

Tala knelt, brushing her fingers over the leaves before gently pulling one free, rubbing it between her fingers. "Yáabitu. Good for coughs, boiled into a tea. Can be used for fever too, but not too much, or it makes the stomach turn inside out."

Tsénatokwa grunted, her approval quiet but clear. "And this one?" She pointed to a taller plant with jagged leaves and clusters of small white blossoms.

Tala plucked one of the leaves and brought it to her nose. "Tupana. Good for stopping bleeding. Best pressed into a wound fresh, but can be dried and ground into a powder for later."

The old woman nodded, watching her closely. "And if a man has eaten something that does not belong in his belly?"

Tala smirked, plucking a plant with dark green, narrow leaves. "Tásipu. Boil it down, make him drink it. He won't be happy, but he'll live."

[CHAPTER 2] — THE HEALER'S TOUCH

Tsénatokwa let out a dry chuckle, kneeling with some effort as she began pulling up the plants by their roots, careful to leave enough behind so they would continue to grow. Tala worked beside her, moving with practiced ease, her fingers wrapping around stems and pulling them free, shaking loose the soil before placing them in her basket.

"You remember well," the old woman said after a moment. "Better than most."

Tala glanced at her, but Tsénatokwa's gaze remained on the plants. It was rare for her to offer such words, and Tala did not take them lightly. She simply nodded and kept working, the rhythm of their task settling into something familiar and steady.

When their baskets were nearly full, they moved toward the creek where the damp soil was rich with burdock root. Tala knelt at the water's edge, using her fingers to dig carefully around the thick, tangled roots before pulling them free. The cold water lapped gently at the bank, the sunlight filtering through the trees casting ripples of light against the surface.

She paused for a moment, glancing down at her reflection.

The water's surface shifted, distorting the lines of her face, but not enough to change what she saw.

Dark hair, the same as her mother's. High cheekbones, sharp like Esihabi's had been. But the eyes—those were not her mother's.

She leaned closer, searching for something she could not name.

Had Esihabi seen herself in her, or had she always been a reminder of the man she lost?

She had never thought to ask. Her mother had loved her fiercely, of that she had no doubt. But had there been moments when she looked at Tala and saw not her daughter, but the man who had ridden away one morning and never returned?

Tala's fingers curled around the root she had been pulling, her knuckles pressing into the damp soil.

It did not matter.

Her mother had chosen to love her, just as her father had chosen to leave.

She tore the root free and placed it in her basket, brushing the dirt from her hands before standing.

That evening, the camp settled into an uneasy stillness. Normally, the air would be filled with laughter, the sound of children playing, the murmured conversations of men and women unwinding after the day's work. But tonight, everything felt restrained, as if the camp itself was waiting, bracing for something unseen. Even the council fire burned lower than usual, its embers pulsing like a slow heartbeat in the center of the gathering space.

Tala sat outside her tipi, her back resting against the packed earth, knees drawn up as she traced invisible shapes against the sky with the tip of her finger. The stars shimmered in the deep black, countless and unchanging, their quiet presence stretching across the heavens as they had since the beginning of time.

[CHAPTER 2] — THE HEALER'S TOUCH

She followed the ones she knew best, the constellations her mother had shown her when she was small, back when everything had felt simpler. The Great Bear, watching over the land. The Twin Hunters, forever chasing their prey across the night sky. The Star Tipi, the place where the spirits gathered when they had finished walking their paths upon the earth.

She lifted her hand, drawing their lines in the air, but no matter how many times she traced them, the stars never formed anything solid, anything she could hold onto. They were distant, shifting only with the slow breath of the seasons, untouchable by the lives of those below.

The future felt the same way.

Like the stars, it stretched before her, uncertain, shifting with the winds of men's choices. She did not know what would come. Would the council decide to fight? Would the settlers press closer, forcing them to defend what land remained? Would she always stand at the edge, caught between two worlds, never fully belonging to either?

Her throat tightened, and she let out a slow breath, bowing her head.

She pressed her palm to the cool earth, grounding herself, feeling the hum of the land beneath her skin. Then, closing her eyes, she let the words slip from her lips, speaking them low, not for any man to hear but for the spirits who moved unseen.

"Taabe nʉmʉnahkahni, nʉ nahkata nʉnʉʉ," she murmured. "Tʉbʉnakʉ nʉ marʉwʉ, nʉ kawatu nʉi."

Great spirits, guide my steps. The path is uncertain, and I cannot see it.

She fell silent, listening to the night, waiting, as if the earth itself might offer some sign, some answer.

A long, aching howl rose from beyond the camp, drifting through the cool air, carrying with it a loneliness so deep it made her shiver. A second howl followed, then silence.

The coyote walked alone tonight.

She swallowed, the sound settling into her bones in a way that made her chest ache. She had heard her mother speak of such things before, of signs woven into the natural world, of messages carried on the wind, in the cries of animals, in the shape of the clouds.

She did not know what it meant, only that it made something inside her feel hollow.

She drew her blanket tighter around her shoulders, tilting her head back to the sky once more.

She had spent her life searching for a place where she truly belonged.

But maybe she was like the coyote, always moving, always searching, never quite at home anywhere.

She closed her eyes, letting the night wash over her, but sleep did not come easily.

[CHAPTER 3] — THE LONE MUSTANG

The following week, the camp awoke to a charged excitement, a restless energy sweeping through like a rising storm. Tala could hear it in the voices that carried through the morning air, the animated tones of warriors speaking in clusters near the council fire, the way even the children ran through the camp with more urgency than usual. She caught bits and pieces of conversation as she passed, the same word repeated again and again—stallion.

She found Tsénatokwa outside the medicine tipi, grinding roots with a careful rhythm. The old woman did not look up as Tala approached, only nodded toward the center of the camp. "They saw it near the river at dawn."

Tala didn't need to ask what. She had already guessed.

A wild stallion.

It had been spoken of for months now, a ghost of the plains, glimpsed only in fleeting moments—black as night, fast as the wind, never captured, never caught. The warriors had tried before, setting traps, attempting to drive it into the stone canyons where escape would be impossible, but each time it had outmaneuvered them. Now, the sighting so close to the camp had reignited the excitement, and men gathered in small knots, discussing their next attempt.

Tala moved closer, stopping where she could listen without drawing attention to herself. A group of warriors stood near the central fire, some crouched, others standing with arms crossed, their voices filled with eager energy.

"It's bigger than I thought," Sawáni was saying, his wounded arm tucked close to his chest, but his grin wide. "I saw it myself. That's no ordinary mustang."

A younger warrior, barely past his first raid, let out a scoff. "They're all the same once you've got a rope on 'em."

Another snorted. "That one? You think a rope will hold it?"

Nāhtöh stepped forward, the men parting slightly as he joined them. His gaze was thoughtful, assessing. "It's not just its speed that's kept it free. It's smart. Knows how to use the land better than the men chasing it."

There were nods of agreement. Tala stayed silent, watching them. She understood why they were drawn to the idea of capturing such a creature. A stallion like that meant strength. Power. To break it would be a sign of skill, a victory over something untamable.

But she saw something else in it.

A creature that had never bowed its head, never accepted reins or saddle, never given itself to any man. It ran because it was meant to, because it knew no other way.

She felt the same.

She turned away, heading toward the food preparations, where women had begun gathering for the evening's feast. The excitement had spread, and it was custom to celebrate before a great hunt or challenge. She crouched beside a woman slicing strips of venison, taking up a basket of corn to grind. The rhythmic motion settled her mind, though she

[CHAPTER 3] — THE LONE MUSTANG

could still hear the warriors nearby, their voices rising and falling in laughter and debate.

Then, clear and cutting through the noise, a voice rang out.

"Maybe Tala should go after it."

Laughter rippled through the group, a few murmured words exchanged. She stiffened, her fingers tightening over the stone grinder. She didn't turn, but she knew who had spoken—Mutsí, a young warrior always looking to prove himself, the kind who found strength in making others seem weak.

"You want to be taken seriously, don't you?" he continued, his tone light, but there was an edge to it. "Seems like a good way to show what you can do."

More laughter, though some of the men only chuckled awkwardly. Others said nothing at all. Tala could feel their gazes shifting toward her, waiting for her to react.

She kept her eyes on her hands, pushing the stone in slow, even circles. She would not let them see it get to her. It was a jest, meant to amuse the men more than anything, but something inside her stirred at the words.

An unspoken challenge.

She did not look up, but she felt it settle deep within her, something sharp and undeniable.

That night, when the camp quieted and the fire burned low, she sat outside her tipi, sharpening her knife in slow, steady strokes. The steel glinted under the moonlight, catching the pale glow as she tested the edge with her thumb.

Then, moving with purpose, she went to her horse, running a hand down its flank, feeling the familiar warmth beneath her palm. She checked the bridle, adjusted the straps, making sure everything was in place.

She would not leave yet. Not tonight.

But soon.

The stallion was out there, running free under the same stars she had traced with her fingers the night before.

And she would find it.

Before dawn, Tala swung onto her horse, the chill of the morning biting through her tunic. The sky stretched vast and endless above her, still painted in the deep blues and purples of night, only the faintest streaks of orange breaking along the horizon. The camp was silent behind her, the embers of the night's fire barely smoldering. No one stirred. This was the best time to leave—before questions, before anyone could talk her out of it.

Her mare shifted beneath her, eager but patient. Tala patted the animal's neck, murmuring a soft reassurance before pressing her knees gently into its sides. The horse started forward, its hooves whispering over the dry earth as they rode out into the open plains.

The air was bracing, crisp against her skin, carrying the scent of damp earth and the distant trace of wild sage. The wind moved through the tall grasses in slow waves, rippling like the surface of a lake. She pulled her blanket tighter around her shoulders, but the cold was already fading as her body warmed with the steady movement of the ride.

[CHAPTER 3] — THE LONE MUSTANG

She kept her gaze low, scanning the ground for signs of her quarry. The stallion had been seen near the river the morning before, and if it had not been disturbed, it might still be roaming the hills beyond. It was not like a normal mustang. This one did not follow predictable paths, did not linger long in any one place. It had learned how to survive on its own, how to outmaneuver those who sought to take it.

Tala understood that instinct better than anyone.

She spotted the tracks just as the sun breached the horizon. The prints were deep, pressed into the damp earth where the stallion had crossed through a narrow stretch of reeds. She pulled her horse to a stop, swinging down with practiced ease, crouching to study the marks.

Fresh.

She reached out, touching the ground, feeling the cool moisture that had not yet been dried by the morning sun. The stallion had passed here not long ago. Its stride was long, purposeful, but it was not running. It had not sensed danger.

Not yet.

She swung back into the saddle, clicking her tongue softly as she urged her mare forward, following the tracks through rolling hills, letting the land guide her. The plains stretched wide and open, the tall grasses swaying, dotted with the occasional stand of trees or a rocky rise. The trail wound through the terrain in a twisting, unpredictable pattern—sometimes cutting straight across open fields, sometimes doubling back toward cover. The mustang did not run without thought. It was clever, aware of its surroundings. It knew how to use the land to its advantage.

Hours passed, the sun climbing higher, and still, she followed. The rhythmic motion of the ride settled into her body, becoming instinct. She did not rush, did not force the chase. This was not about overpowering the stallion. It was about understanding it.

By midday, she caught sight of movement near a rocky outcrop in the distance.

She reined in her horse, keeping low, her breath slowing. The stallion stood at the edge of the rise, its coat dark as the night that had just faded, the muscles beneath its hide shifting with every slight movement. It grazed lazily, unaware or unconcerned with her presence. Its tail flicked, ears twitching as it kept watch on the land around it.

Tala dismounted, her heartbeat steady but strong.

She moved carefully, her steps slow, her body low to the ground. The wind was in her favor, carrying her scent away rather than toward the stallion.

"Taabe nʉmʉ," she murmured softly, the words barely more than a breath. "You run because the wind calls you, because the land is yours alone."

The mustang lifted its head, nostrils flaring, ears pricked forward. It did not move, but its muscles tensed, prepared to bolt.

Tala took another step.

The air between them felt stretched tight, like the moment before a storm breaks. She could feel the weight of it, the unspoken understanding between them. This was not just a horse. This was something untamed, something that did not belong to anyone—not the warriors who wanted to break it, not the land that tried to hold it.

Just like her.

She reached out, her fingers hovering inches from the stallion's flank, her heart pounding with a strange, unfamiliar thrill.

The mustang snorted sharply, eyes flashing, and in an instant, it bolted.

Tala barely had time to react before the stallion was gone, hooves tearing up the earth, muscles rippling as it sprinted into the distance, its black form a blur against the golden plains.

She let out a breath, frustration curling in her chest—but beneath it, something else stirred.

Not disappointment.

Something wilder.

Something freer.

She had felt it in that moment before the stallion fled, in the tension between them, in the weight of its presence so close to hers. A thrill unlike anything she had known in a long time—sharp and electric, stirring something deep in her chest. It was not just the nearness of the animal, not just the challenge of the chase, but something more. A connection, fleeting but undeniable. A wildness that called to her, recognizing something kindred in her soul. For that brief instant, she had not been an outsider, not half of one thing and half of another, but something whole, something untethered, something that did not answer to anyone. Then it was gone, lost in the wind and the pounding of hooves, but the feeling remained, coursing through her veins like fire.

Tala rode back toward the camp as the sun dipped low over the horizon, casting the plains in hues of deep amber and purple. The ride was long, the weight of exhaustion settling into her limbs, but her mind refused to still. Dust clung to her skin, mixing with the dried sweat on her brow, and her legs ached from the hours in the saddle. Yet none of it mattered.

She could still feel the stallion's presence, as if its wild spirit had pressed itself into her bones. That brief moment before it fled, when she had felt something raw, untamed, something that called to her in a way nothing else had before—it still burned in her chest. It was more than just a challenge, more than proving herself to the warriors who had mocked her. It was something she could not yet name, but it made her stomach twist and her pulse quicken.

By the time she reached the camp, the evening fires had been lit, their glow flickering against the darkened sky. People moved about in quiet conversation, the energy from the stallion's sighting still lingering in the air. She slid from her horse with stiff legs, brushing dust from her tunic, and led her mare to water before heading toward the fire where some of the elders had gathered.

She settled near the edge of the circle, letting the warmth seep into her aching muscles. Voices rose and fell in quiet discussion, but it was not until an old man spoke that true silence fell over the group. It was Tuhubut, a man known for his stories, his voice worn with age but still steady as the land itself. Tala had heard his stories many times

[CHAPTER 3] — THE LONE MUSTANG

growing up, but tonight, something about his presence felt heavier, as if his words carried more weight.

"You know of the lone wolf?" Tuhubut said, poking at the fire with his staff, stirring embers into the air. "Not the one that runs with his pack. No, I speak of the one who roams alone, never belonging to one place, never taking a mate."

Some of the younger warriors leaned in, drawn to the sound of his voice, the way it wove through the night air.

"He was once strong, this wolf," the elder continued. "A great hunter, swift, cunning. He ran with his brothers, fought beside them, shared in their kills. But one day, the spirits sent him a test. A great elk, strong and fierce, appeared on the land, one that no man or beast had been able to catch. The wolf felt the call in his blood, the need to prove himself. He left his pack behind, chasing the elk, running for days and nights, through rivers, over hills, across frozen ground. Each time he drew close, the elk would leap away, always just beyond his reach."

Tala watched the fire, listening, the warmth pressing against her skin.

"His brothers called for him to return," Tuhubut went on, his eyes flicking to the men gathered before him. "But the wolf did not stop. He could not. He had tasted the chase, and nothing else felt real. But the elk was never meant to be caught, not by him. It was a spirit, placed there to test the wolf's heart. And when the wolf finally stopped running, he turned back to find that his pack was gone. Seasons had passed, his place among them lost. He had run so far, for so long, that the only thing left for him was the trail beneath his

[CHAPTER 3] — THE LONE MUSTANG

feet. And so, he wandered, forever chasing something that would never be his."

Silence settled over the fire, the crackling of the flames the only sound between them.

Tala did not move. The words settled deep inside her, twisting in ways she did not understand.

A lone creature, always running, never belonging.

Was that her fate? Had she been chasing something all this time—acceptance, a place to belong—only to find herself destined to wander, always just outside the life she longed for?

She pulled her blanket tighter around her shoulders, the unease sitting heavy in her chest.

When she finally slipped away from the fire and settled inside her tipi, sleep did not come easily.

The moment her eyes closed; she was running.

The dream came alive, vivid as the waking world. The land stretched before her in endless waves of golden grass, the wind whipping through her hair, the earth pounding beneath her feet. But she was not alone. The stallion was there, its black coat gleaming under a sky filled with stars, its mane wild and flowing as it raced ahead.

She chased it, her breath coming fast, her limbs burning with effort, but she did not stop. The air rushed past her, the thrill of the chase surging through her veins, but no matter how hard she pushed forward, the stallion remained just beyond her reach.

She called out to it, though her voice was lost to the wind.

[CHAPTER 3] — THE LONE MUSTANG

The stallion turned its head, its dark eyes catching hers for a brief moment, and in them, she saw herself—not the girl sitting at the edges of her people, not the healer's apprentice, not the half-blood always caught between two worlds. She saw something free, something untamed, something that did not answer to anyone.

The horse let out a snort and surged forward, faster, the distance between them growing. She pushed herself harder, reaching, straining, but the harder she ran, the farther away it seemed to be.

The land stretched on, endless.

Her breath hitched, her legs faltering, but she kept going, even as her body screamed for rest.

Then the land shifted, the sky above shifting with it, the stars swirling into patterns she did not recognize. The stallion reared, pawing at the sky, and for a brief moment, she thought she saw something behind it—something vast, something waiting.

Then it was gone.

She woke before dawn, the silence of the tipi pressing in around her.

The dream still clung to her, her breath uneven, her heart racing as if she had truly been running. She lay still, staring into the darkness, her mind filled with a single question.

Was she meant to chase something she would never catch?

[CHAPTER 4] — A PLACE AT THE FIRE

A month later, the morning air carried a sharpness that had not been there the day before, a crisp bite that crept through the grass and settled deep in the lungs. The heat of summer had faded, and with it came the restless energy of the changing season. The leaves on the distant cottonwoods had begun to turn brittle and golden, and the wind, once thick with the scent of sun-warmed earth, now carried the promise of frost. Autumn had arrived.

The camp moved with purpose, a shift in rhythm as the people prepared for the long months ahead. Men worked together, lashing wooden poles tighter against the tipis, reinforcing them against the coming snow. Smoke curled from cooking fires as women roasted strips of meat before hanging them to dry, their voices rising and falling in steady conversation. The younger children gathered fallen wood, laughing as they carried bundles twice their size, while the elders supervised, their sharp eyes missing nothing.

Tala had grown up in this way of life, had watched the same preparations unfold year after year, yet each time, the change of season unsettled something deep inside her. The work was familiar, but the feeling of belonging was not.

She crouched beside a fresh kill, a large buck that had been brought in from the hunt that morning. The warmth had already left its body, its lifeblood drained into the earth. Her knife slid easily through the hide as she worked to separate it from the muscle beneath, her movements swift, efficient. She knew this task well—her mother had taught her before she could even hold a blade properly, guiding her hands with patience, showing her how to be precise, to be sure.

Yet as she worked, she became aware of the others around her. The women moved in perfect rhythm, their hands deft, their coordination effortless. They did not need to speak to one another to know what came next, did not need to pause or look up. They had done this together so many times that their movements were second nature, a silent understanding woven between them.

Tala was skilled, but she did not move as they did.

She continued her work, focused on the task before her, but she could feel the quiet glances. The way the women worked around her rather than with her. They did not do it intentionally, she knew. It was not an act of rejection, not something meant to wound. It was simply the way things were. They belonged to one another in a way she never fully had.

She had done this work for years, had proven herself capable time and again. But some things could not be earned with skill alone.

A voice broke through her thoughts. "You are quick with a knife."

Tala glanced up to find Nahwun, a girl near her age, kneeling beside her with a slight smile. She had always been kind, never one to speak against Tala, though never one to speak for her either.

Tala nodded. "I was taught well."

[CHAPTER 4] — A PLACE AT THE FIRE

Nahwun passed her a fresh strip of meat to place on the drying rack. "That is clear."

The warmth in her voice was genuine, and Tala felt the tightness in her chest loosen just slightly. But as she reached for the next cut, another glance caught her eye—this one not so kind.

Piam, a woman a few years older, worked with the others, her hands moving swiftly, but her gaze flicked toward Tala with something unreadable. Not outright disdain, but doubt. A question that had never been spoken but had always been there.

Tala knew what it meant.

Was she truly one of them?

She pressed her lips together and kept working, her hands steady, her posture unbent.

Her skills should speak for themselves. She knew that.

But the sting of exclusion still lingered, just beneath the surface, a quiet ache that never quite went away.

That evening, as the fires crackled and cast their glow against the gathering darkness, the camp settled into a familiar rhythm of stories and laughter. Warriors sat near the flames, recounting their own past hunts and battles, their voices rising and falling with pride and amusement. The younger ones leaned in close, their eyes wide with admiration, eager to hear of great deeds and near escapes.

Tala sat toward the edge of the gathering, where she often found herself, close enough to listen, far enough to feel separate. She let her gaze drift over the faces illuminated by the fire's flickering light, watching the way the men spoke

[CHAPTER 4] — A PLACE AT THE FIRE

with their whole bodies, how they reenacted the moments of their fights, mimicking the movements of the hunt or the strike of a blade. It was a familiar sight, one that made the air hum with energy.

Then, as the laughter faded and a comfortable silence settled, Tuhubut lifted his staff and cleared his throat. The old man's voice carried with the weight of time, and as always, when he spoke, the camp listened.

"You have heard the tales of our people," he began, his gaze sweeping over those gathered. "You know of our wars, of our hunts, of the blood that has been spilled to keep this land ours. But have you heard of the battle against the Apache, when the warriors of our people faced death and did not falter?"

A murmur ran through the crowd, a shifting of bodies as everyone settled in closer.

Tuhubut's voice deepened, taking on the slow, measured rhythm of a storyteller. "Long ago, before the seasons wore deep into my bones, before even the fathers of the men here were born, the Apache roamed these lands. They were strong, and they believed these lands were theirs. They did not yet know that the Numunuu had come to ride the wind, that we had taken the horse as our own and could strike like the storm itself."

Tala's breath stilled, her fingers pressing into the earth beneath her as she listened.

"They came from the south," Tuhubut continued, "a war party of fifty men, their weapons sharp, their spirits high, for they thought they would drive us away as they had driven others before. But they did not know of Isatai."

[CHAPTER 4] — A PLACE AT THE FIRE

A few nodded at the name, some shifting with knowing glances.

"Isatai was not just a warrior—he was the kind of man the spirits favor, the kind who sees not just with his eyes, but with the heart of the land itself. He knew the Apache would come. He had seen the signs, the way the birds moved, the way the wind carried a new scent. He gathered his warriors—not many, no more than twenty—and they rode to meet the enemy before they could strike."

The fire popped, sending a spray of embers into the night.

"The Apache did not fear them. They saw twenty against fifty and believed they had already won. But Isatai did not fight as they did. He did not wait to be struck first. When the battle came, he led his men in circles, moving like the spirits themselves, appearing and disappearing with the rise of the dust, striking from nowhere and vanishing before the Apache could turn their blades."

Tuhubut's hands moved as he spoke, his fingers curling like the rush of hooves, the wind of war.

"The Apache grew angry, impatient. They broke their formation, and that was when Isatai struck. He split his warriors into two, one half driving the Apache forward, the other waiting among the rocks, hidden. And when the Apache thought they were chasing men who fled in fear, they found themselves surrounded instead."

A few warriors grinned. nodding at the cleverness of the maneuver.

[CHAPTER 4] — A PLACE AT THE FIRE

"The battle was swift. The Apache, trapped, had nowhere to run. The ground turned red beneath them, and their leader fell beneath Isatai's lance. Those who lived did not stay to fight again. They ran south, back to the deserts where they belonged, and we did not see them again for many seasons. That was the day the N~~u~~mun~~uu~~ claimed this land, the day we showed the Apache that the wind does not belong to them."

The story ended, but the silence it left in its wake was thick, filled with the weight of something greater than words.

Tala felt it deep in her chest, a pulse, an ache, something she had no name for.

The blood of warriors ran through her veins. She had heard the stories all her life, of battles fought, lands claimed, enemies driven away. And yet she had never truly felt as if she were part of them. She was no warrior. She had no battle of her own.

But she wanted to.

She wanted to be part of something greater, something that would outlast her.

As the fire crackled and the voices of the camp rose again in conversation, she sat quietly, staring into the flames, feeling the weight of the story settle inside her.

The past was written in the words of men like T~~u~~h~~u~~b~~u~~t.

But what of her future?

Would anyone ever speak her name with the same reverence? Or would she forever remain just outside of the stories, watching but never written into them?

[CHAPTER 4] — A PLACE AT THE FIRE

The fire had burned low, its embers glowing deep orange, pulsing like the heart of the camp. Conversation had settled into a comfortable lull, warriors shifting in their seats, some sharpening knives, others gazing into the flickering flames, lost in thought. The weight of Tuhubut's story still hung in the air, the lingering awe of battle and victory, of warriors whose names had been woven into the history of their people.

Tala hesitated, glancing around the fire, her fingers pressing against her knee. She had never spoken here, not like this. The stories were for the warriors, for the men who had earned the right to tell them. But her mother's voice stirred in her memory, the soft lilt of it, the way she would spin words like the wind itself, making even the simplest tale feel like something powerful.

She drew in a slow breath.

"My mother once told me a story," she said, her voice steady but quiet. "One of the wind and the trickster Coyote."

A few heads turned. Some glanced at her, others barely gave her a second look. She swallowed down the doubt rising in her chest and continued.

"There was a time when the wind did not run free. It belonged to an old woman, high in the mountains, who kept it tied up in a great bag inside her tipi. Without the wind, the world stood still. The grass did not sway, the trees did not sing, and the birds could not lift their wings. Everything was trapped in silence, waiting."

Nahwun, still seated near her, tilted her head slightly, listening. A young boy leaned forward, resting his chin on

[CHAPTER 4] — A PLACE AT THE FIRE

his arms. Tala felt the smallest flicker of encouragement, so she pressed on.

"But Coyote did not like waiting. He was clever, and more than that, he was impatient. He saw the birds struggling, saw the stillness in the land, and thought, 'This is not the way things should be.' So he decided to set the wind free."

A few warriors chuckled knowingly—Coyote was always a fool as much as he was cunning. Tala allowed a small smile and continued.

"He climbed high into the mountains, finding the old woman's tipi where she sat guarding the great bag of wind. She was wise, and she did not trust him, but Coyote was clever. He flattered her, told her he had traveled far just to see such a strong and beautiful keeper of the wind. She laughed and let him inside."

Someone near the fire snorted, muttering, "Always full of words, that Coyote."

Tala nodded slightly, meeting the man's eye. "Yes. But sometimes, words are not enough."

She shifted her weight, her fingers curling slightly in the dirt. "Coyote sat with the old woman, keeping her talking, distracting her. While she spoke, he crept closer to the bag. Just as she turned away for a moment, he lunged forward, grabbing the rope and tearing it free."

Her hands mimicked the motion, fingers pulling at invisible knots, caught up in the telling now.

"The bag flew open, and the wind rushed out with a great howl, tearing through the tipi, sweeping across the mountains, racing down into the valley below. The trees bent, the grass swayed, the birds took flight for the first time in moons. The wind was free again!"

A few of the younger boys grinned, the idea of such mischief lighting their eyes.

"But," Tala said, pausing, lowering her voice just enough to draw them in, "Coyote had not thought of what the wind would do to him."

Silence settled for a moment. The embers crackled.

"The wind was wild from being trapped so long. It did not thank Coyote. Instead, it grabbed him, lifted him high into the sky, spinning him end over end, tossing him across the land like a dry leaf. He tumbled down the mountains, across the plains, rolling and rolling, until at last he crashed into the dirt, too dizzy to stand."

Laughter rippled through the group, a few warriors shaking their heads at the trickster's folly.

"And that," Tala finished, letting herself smile, "is why the wind still howls when it runs through the mountains. It is laughing, remembering how it sent Coyote tumbling."

She had barely finished the last words when a scoffing voice cut through the moment.

"You tell it well," Mutsí said, leaning back on his elbows. "But do you even understand the weight of such stories?"

The laughter that had come so easily moments before shifted, turning uneasy. Tala stiffened, her stomach knotting.

[CHAPTER 4] — A PLACE AT THE FIRE

"These tales are not just for amusement," he continued, gesturing toward her. "They teach. They carry meaning, passed down from those before us. Do you think speaking the words makes them yours?"

A few chuckled in agreement, though others only looked away, unwilling to be caught in it. Tala felt heat rush to her face, her throat tightening.

She had known this moment would come, had braced for it. And yet, it still burned.

Her mother's stories had been hers, had been spoken to her in the same way warriors passed down their own knowledge. And yet, to them, it would never be enough.

She swallowed, jaw tight.

Without a word, she pushed to her feet, stepping back from the fire. The warmth that had felt inviting moments before now only made her feel like she could not breathe.

She walked past the tipis, past the groups of men still murmuring among themselves, past the women who had begun to gather near the cooking fires, where the smell of roasting meat drifted in the cool air. She did not stop until she reached the edge of the camp, where the land stretched wide and open, the sky vast above her.

The stars shone in endless waves, bright and unmoving. They did not care who she was. They did not question whether she belonged.

She wrapped her arms around herself, breathing in the cool air, steadying her thoughts.

Why did she still fight for their acceptance?

[CHAPTER 4] — A PLACE AT THE FIRE

Why did she still yearn for something that might never come?

The wind stirred through the grass, rushing past her, moving on without hesitation.

For a moment, she closed her eyes and let it pull at her, wondering if, like Coyote, she, too, had misjudged her own strength.

Tala finally turned away from the vast night sky, the weight of her thoughts pressing heavy against her ribs. The wind had carried her far, but it could not tell her where she belonged. With a slow breath, she made her way back toward the camp, her steps quiet against the earth. The fires still burned low, their glow flickering against the tipis, casting long shapes that stretched and shifted with the movement of those still awake. She moved toward her own tipi, the place that had always been hers yet never truly felt like home.

Tala sat outside her tipi, the cool night air brushing against her skin, though she barely felt it. She did not hear Tsénatokwa approach, but she felt the shift in the air, the presence of the old woman settling beside her with the patience of one who had lived many seasons. Tsénatokwa did not speak right away, did not ask why Tala had pulled herself away from the others. She only sat, her bones creaking slightly as she eased onto the earth, her weathered hands resting lightly in her lap.

The silence stretched, comfortable, unhurried. Tala had always admired that about Tsénatokwa—her ability to let stillness speak when others filled it with needless words.

[CHAPTER 4] — A PLACE AT THE FIRE

After a long moment, the old woman exhaled softly, then began to speak.

"There was once a woman," Tsénatokwa said, her voice low and steady, carrying the weight of something ancient. "Born of two rivers, two bloods, flowing from two peoples before there were names for them. She was not of one camp, not of one tipi—she walked between the ways of her mother's people and her father's, but neither side claimed her fully."

Tala turned her head slightly, drawn in despite herself.

"This woman was not Comanche, nor was she of any single people. She was simply herself. But to those who looked upon her, that was not enough."

The fire crackled softly, casting long shapes that flickered with the wind. The night moved on around them, life continuing as it always had, as it always would. But Tala sat still, listening.

Tsénatokwa picked up a small twig and rolled it between her fingers. "She tried to be both. She learned the ways of her mother's people—the songs that called the buffalo, the prayers that carried strength to the hunters, the ways of healing passed down from the grandmothers before her. But still, they did not see her as one of them. She learned the ways of her father's kin—the skill of the bow, the secrets of the old trails that stretched far beyond the land she had known. But still, she was neither one nor the other."

Tala swallowed, a tightness growing in her chest.

"So, she left," Tsénatokwa continued, lifting her gaze toward the sky. "Not in anger, not in fear, but because the

[CHAPTER 4] — A PLACE AT THE FIRE

land called her. She walked beyond the camps, beyond the places where names held meaning, and she let the land itself tell her who she was."

Tala frowned slightly, shifting where she sat. "The land?"

Tsénatokwa nodded. "The land does not ask where you came from. It does not care what name was given to you at birth or whether one tipi claims you or another turns you away. It only asks if you know how to listen."

She pressed the twig into the dirt, drawing slow, deliberate lines. "She walked alone for many seasons, but she did not wander without purpose. She learned to read the river's song, to watch the clouds and know what was coming before it arrived. She did not wait for others to tell her where she belonged. She built her own fire, made her own place, and when the time came, people sought her—not because she had changed, not because she had become one of them, but because she had made something of her own, something strong, something that could not be ignored."

Tala's breath was slow, measured. She could feel the weight of the story pressing against her ribs, settling deep in places she had not let herself acknowledge before.

Tsénatokwa turned her head, studying her in the dim light. "You listen to stories, but you do not yet see your own place within them. You think fire is only warmth, only something that belongs to others who sit around it. But fire is more than that. Fire is a place of belonging. It is a thing that must be built, tended, shaped by the hands that feed it."

[CHAPTER 4] — A PLACE AT THE FIRE

She reached out, touching Tala's arm lightly, her fingers firm but not unkind. "You must build your own fire, Tala. Even if it is not among the others."

The words settled over her like a blanket—warm, comforting, but carrying weight.

Tsénatokwa rose slowly, her movements unhurried. "You will learn," she said simply, then turned, disappearing into the night as quietly as she had come.

Tala sat there for a long time, staring at the stars, feeling something shift deep inside her, something that had nothing to do with the old ache of wanting to belong.

She would not beg for acceptance.

She would not keep reaching for a place that did not want her.

She would carve her own place, build her own fire, even if it meant standing alone.

And as the embers in the camp crackled, carrying stories she no longer felt a part of, she knew—her journey was only beginning.

[CHAPTER 5] — SHADOWS ON THE HORIZON

A week had passed since Tsénatokwa's story, but the words still lingered in Tala's mind, pressing against her thoughts like a stone caught in the river's current. The camp had carried on, preparing for the winter, but the unease in the air had not faded. The scouts had not reported any new threats, yet the feeling remained, a quiet warning carried on the wind.

Before the sun had fully risen, the first sounds of approaching hooves shattered the stillness of morning. Riders galloped into the camp, their ponies kicking up dirt, their urgency sending a ripple of tension through the camp. Women straightened from their morning tasks, warriors turned from tending their weapons, and the air grew thick with unspoken questions.

Tala stood near the healer's tipi, watching as the dust-covered men dismounted, their faces tight with urgency. One of them, Pauhtan, a seasoned scout, strode toward the gathering warriors, his expression grim.

"They come," he said, his breath still heavy from the ride. "More than before."

A murmur swept through the gathered men, a rustling of movement as warriors closed in, their faces darkening.

"Where?" someone demanded.

[CHAPTER 5] — SHADOWS ON THE HORIZON

"Near the river," Pauhtan answered. "Closer than we've seen them. They do not move like hunters. They move like men preparing for war."

The murmur became a growl, the weight of his words settling over the camp like a storm rolling in. Tala felt her pulse quicken. She had known this was coming, known it the moment she first heard the scouts speak of settlers moving north. But knowing did not make it easier.

Warriors gathered quickly, their voices rising in heated discussion. Some spoke of moving the camp, of pulling back before they were surrounded. Others clenched their fists around their weapons, eyes burning with the fire of men unwilling to run.

Nāhtöh stepped forward, his stance rigid, his gaze fierce. "We do not wait for them to come to us," he said, his voice sharp with conviction. "We strike first."

A few warriors grunted in agreement. Others looked uneasy.

"Wait for what?" Nāhtöh continued, his arms crossing over his chest. "For them to build their houses on our land? To bring their rifles, their sickness, their hunger for what is not theirs? If we let them settle, we will be the ones running."

A young warrior, Piahka, nodded. "Better to strike while we still hold the ground."

But an older man, Wauki, shook his head. "You think their numbers are small now, but how many more will come? We kill them, and their people will not forget. They will bring more."

"They will come whether we fight or not," Nāhtöh shot back.

The debate grew louder, voices clashing like blades. Tala stayed on the edge, listening, her heart pounding. She knew how the settlers thought. Her mother had spoken of it often, of how they measured land in ownership, not belonging. Of how they built fences not just to keep their animals in, but to keep others out. If the warriors attacked now, it would not be a battle—it would be the first spark of a fire that could not be put out.

She wanted to say so, to speak what she knew. But her place was not among them. Not in this.

Instead, she studied their faces, their stances. Even those who called for war held tension in their shoulders, a flicker of uncertainty in their eyes. These were warriors who had fought before, who had seen what steel and lead could do. They did not fear battle, but they knew the cost.

Tobáhā had been silent throughout, his expression unreadable as he let the men argue. Finally, he lifted a hand, and the voices stilled.

"War is not won by haste," he said, his voice slow, measured. "It is won by knowing when to strike and when to wait. The land does not belong to those who rush into battle. It belongs to those who endure."

Nāhtöh's jaw tightened. 'And how long do we endure before we have nothing left?"

Tobáhā turned his gaze to the scout. "They have moved closer, but have they attacked?"

Pauhtan shook his head. "No. Not yet."

[CHAPTER 5] — SHADOWS ON THE HORIZON

"Then we wait." Tobáhá's gaze swept over the gathered warriors. "We watch. If they mean to take what is ours, we will answer. But we do not strike blindly."

A few men grumbled, but none openly challenged him. Tala could feel the frustration rolling off Náhtöh, but even he did not defy the chief's word.

Tala let out a slow breath. The decision had been made—for now. But the tension in the camp had not eased. The storm was still coming.

She only hoped they would be ready.

The camp did not settle as it should have that night. The usual rhythm of voices, of murmured conversations and the soft laughter of children drifting into sleep, was absent. Instead, there was a weight in the air, thick and unspoken, pressing down on everyone like a storm waiting to break. Warriors sat near the fires, sharpening blades that had already tasted blood, their faces drawn tight with thoughts they did not share. The older men spoke in low tones, their eyes dark with knowing. Even the women, who often carried the strength of the camp through every season, moved with a quiet purpose, their gazes shifting toward the men, toward their sons, toward the place where decisions had been made but no one felt at peace with them.

Tala sat near the healer's fire, staring into the flames. The flickering light cast long shapes against the tipis, twisting, shifting, changing form with each breath of the wind. She had seen fire move like this before—her mother had once said that flames could speak if one knew how to listen. But tonight, she did not understand what they were saying. The shapes danced like omens, stretching too far,

[CHAPTER 5] — SHADOWS ON THE HORIZON

curling too high, flickering and shifting like things that could not be held.

Her stomach tightened. She could not shake the feeling that the land itself was waiting.

After some time, she rose, moving through the quiet spaces of the camp, past warriors sitting with their heads bent close, past women grinding corn who did not speak to one another as they usually would. She stepped into her tipi, pulling the blanket around her shoulders, lying down but finding no comfort in the familiar place.

Sleep did not come easily. She closed her eyes, listening to the distant sounds of the wind threading through the plains, the restless murmur of the camp, the crackle of fire. Her mind was too full, her thoughts running in circles, never settling. And yet, at some point, sleep took her.

And in sleep, her mother came.

She stood at the edge of a great river, her form blurred by the mist rising from the water. The river was vast, wider than any Tala had ever seen, its surface dark and shifting, deep with stories and things unspoken. Esihabi's dark hair lifted in the unseen wind, her face calm but heavy with something Tala could not name.

Tala stepped forward. "Ina?" The word felt thick in her throat, unsure, as if she had forgotten how to say it.

Esihabi lifted her gaze, her dark eyes meeting Tala's with something deep, something knowing. She did not move closer, did not cross the river that separated them.

"The river is rising." Her voice was steady, certain.

[CHAPTER 5] — SHADOWS ON THE HORIZON

Tala frowned. She could not see it, could not feel the water moving, yet her mother's words carried weight. "What does it mean?"

Esihabi looked down at the water, then back at Tala. "It is coming."

Tala's pulse quickened. The mist thickened around them, curling up from the water's edge, swallowing the land behind her mother so that nothing remained but Esihabi and the dark, shifting river. "I don't understand."

Esihabi's gaze did not waver. "You will."

Tala took another step forward, reaching out, but her mother did not reach back. Instead, her face softened, something quiet and mournful flickering in her expression.

"You must not stand in the current." The words were heavy, like stones sinking into the riverbed.

A gust of wind swept through, lifting Esihabi's hair, her figure shifting with the mist, and then—she was gone.

The river remained, deep and endless, stretching into the darkness, but there was no one on the other side.

Tala's breath hitched, panic lacing through her. She stepped forward again, but the ground beneath her feet was already slipping, the world tilting, the river stretching wider, pulling away.

She reached, but there was nothing left to grasp.

The mist thickened, swallowing everything.

She woke with a sharp breath, her heart pounding in her chest, the feeling of loss curling through her like a wound freshly opened.

[CHAPTER 5] — SHADOWS ON THE HORIZON

Dawn had not yet come. The camp was still dark, the fire outside her tipi reduced to glowing embers.

Tala sat up, wrapping her arms around herself, her breath unsteady. The dream clung to her, thick and unshakable. It had not felt like a dream at all. It had felt like something else.

Something coming.

She pressed her fingers against her temples, trying to calm her racing thoughts. But the words would not leave her.

You must not stand in the current.

She had no idea what it meant.

But deep in her bones, she knew—something terrible was coming.

Leaving her tipi, the air was sharp with the bite of morning cold, the kind that clung to the skin and seeped into the bones before the sun could chase it away. It carried the distant sounds of warriors preparing for what may come— the scrape of stone against metal as blades were honed, the low rumble of voices as men spoke in hushed, clipped tones, the restless stamping of horses sensing the tension in the air. Fires burned low, their embers glowing beneath the weight of the coming day.

Tala sat down outside her tipi, a whetstone in one hand, her knife in the other. The blade caught the faintest trace of light as she worked, the steady rhythm of stone against steel grounding her in the task. She knew this knife as well as she knew her own hands. It had been hers for years, its grip molded to the shape of her palm, the edge honed sharp enough to slice clean through sinew and bone. She had used

[CHAPTER 5] — SHADOWS ON THE HORIZON

it to skin deer, to carve meat, to cut leather and sinew for stitching, but never for what the warriors prepared for now.

Her fingers curled around the handle, feeling the weight of it, testing the balance. If the fighting reached them, if the white men came, would she be able to use it? Not to cut or prepare, but to take a life?

She had been trained in survival. She knew how to track, how to move unseen, how to fight when there was no other choice. But knowing and doing were two different things. She had seen the aftermath of battle, the wounds that did not heal, the silence that followed when warriors did not return.

She swallowed, dragging the stone across the blade again, forcing herself to focus. It was not a matter of what she wanted. It was a matter of what might be necessary.

The sky shifted above her, deep indigo beginning to lighten at the edges, streaked with the first pale traces of dawn. It was a quiet thing, this slow unraveling of night, but it felt different today. Heavier. As if the land itself was holding its breath. Tala stared at the horizon, wondering if this would be the last time the world felt unchanged.

She had spent her life walking between two places, trying to balance on ground that was never steady beneath her feet. She had fought to carve a place for herself, to prove that she belonged in a world that had never quite accepted her. But now, everything was shifting, slipping through her fingers like water, refusing to be held.

She did not know what the day would bring.

She only knew that something was coming.

[CHAPTER 5] — SHADOWS ON THE HORIZON

Drawing in a slow breath, she set down the whetstone and rose to her feet. The cold pressed against her skin, but she barely felt it now. She stood there, shoulders straight, chin lifted, looking at the sky and bracing herself for the storm that was about to break

[CHAPTER 6] — BLOOD AND ASHES

The first sign of destruction came with the smoke. It rose against the pale morning sky, dark and thick, twisting in unnatural columns that did not belong. Tala saw it from the edge of the camp, where she had gone to fetch water. At first, it could have been anything—a distant fire, a careless hunter burning dry grass—but deep down, she knew. This was not a campfire. It was not a cooking fire. It was something far worse.

She turned back toward the center of the camp, her heart pounding, just as a distant pounding of hooves grew louder. A scout burst into the clearing, his pony lathered in sweat, his face streaked with dust. He barely had time to pull the horse to a stop before he threw himself from the saddle.

"They came!" His voice cracked from breathlessness and urgency. "Soldiers—they attacked! The camp is gone!"

A stunned silence fell over the gathered people, but only for a breath. Then came the rush—the sharp intake of gasps, the murmur of voices swelling like a rising wind. Warriors surged forward, demanding answers, their hands tightening around weapons. Women clutched their children, their eyes wide with fear.

Tobáhā stepped forward, his expression hard. "Where?"

The scout swallowed, his chest heaving. "Not far. Half a day's ride south, near the river. They came in the night. Rifles—so many rifles." His voice wavered, as if he still saw

[CHAPTER 6] — BLOOD AND ASHES

it, the flashes of gunfire in the dark. "We tried to fight. But—" His throat bobbed. "Many are dead. The rest scattered."

Nähtöh's face darkened, his fists clenching at his sides. "How many soldiers?"

"More than before," the scout answered. "They did not come to talk. They came to kill."

Anger rippled through the camp like a wildfire catching dry grass. Warriors moved quickly, some rushing to gather weapons, others calling for their horses. The women moved just as swiftly, packing food, preparing for what they all knew was coming.

Tala stood among them, watching as men prepared for battle, for revenge. But she would not be among them. She already knew her place.

She turned toward the healer's tipi, pushing aside the flap and stepping inside. The air smelled of herbs, of dried plants hanging from the poles, of earth and ash. Without hesitation, she moved to the bundles of supplies, her hands already in motion. She did not have the luxury of rage—her duty would be tending to the aftermath.

Tsénatokwa entered behind her, silent but steady, her wrinkled hands already reaching for supplies. "You know there will be wounded."

Tala nodded. "Yes."

Tsénatokwa's eyes, dark and sharp, flicked toward the entrance. "You do not wish to fight."

Tala's hands stilled over a roll of bandages. "I don't know if I could."

[CHAPTER 6] — BLOOD AND ASHES

The old woman studied her for a long moment before nodding. "Then your hands will serve where others cannot." There was no judgment, only certainty.

Outside, the warriors were mounting up. The camp was filled with the sharp sounds of hooves stamping, the tightening of bowstrings, the low murmurs of men preparing for battle. And then, with a final command from Tobáhā, they rode. A dust cloud rose in their wake, swallowing them from sight.

The camp was left in uneasy silence.

Hours passed in waiting, in preparation. Tala did not stop moving. She pounded herbs into salves, boiled water, rolled bandages tight. She tried not to think about the men who had ridden out. Tried not to wonder how many would return.

Then the survivors came.

First, it was a small figure on horseback, barely holding onto the reins. Then another, stumbling on foot, clutching a wounded arm. And then more—women, children, and a few warriors, their faces hollowed by pain and exhaustion.

Tala ran to meet them, her feet barely touching the earth. A child collapsed into the arms of an elder, sobbing. A warrior sagged against his horse, his side slick with blood. A woman walked with empty eyes, clutching nothing in her hands but air.

Tala fell to her knees beside the first wounded man, tearing fabric away from a bullet wound, pressing down hard to stop the bleeding. Blood soaked her hands, warm and thick, but she did not hesitate. She cleaned wounds, spread

[CHAPTER 6] — BLOOD AND ASHES

salves, whispered quiet reassurances to those who trembled beneath her touch.

A woman collapsed beside her, her face streaked with soot and tears. Her hands grasped Tala's, fingers digging into her skin. "The world is changing," she choked out. "Nothing will stay as it was."

Tala froze, the words slamming into her like a blow to the chest.

The woman's grip tightened. "Do you understand?" Her voice cracked. "Do you see it?"

Tala could not answer.

Because she did see it.

She had seen it in her dreams. In the river, in the mist, in her mother's warning. The land itself had tried to tell her.

She just did not know what it meant.

That night, the fire burned low in the center of the camp, its glow flickering against the faces of those gathered around it. The air was thick with smoke and sorrow, the weight of the day pressing down on them all. The survivors of the attack had been tended to, their wounds bandaged, their grief given space to settle, but there was no peace in the camp tonight. There could not be.

The council had been called. Warriors sat in a tight circle, their faces hard, their bodies tense. Elders sat among them, their expressions heavy with the knowledge of what war had cost them before. Around them, others lingered just beyond the reach of the firelight—women, younger men, those who would not speak but who still wanted to hear. Tala

[CHAPTER 6] — BLOOD AND ASHES

stood at the edge, arms crossed, her fingers digging into her own skin as she watched.

Nähtöh was the first to speak, and there was no mistaking the fury in his voice. "We cannot let this pass." He did not sit as he spoke, but stood, his broad chest rising and falling with the force of his anger. "The soldiers came, and they will come again. They burned our camp, killed our people. And for what? Because they want us gone. Because they think they can take what is ours." He swept his gaze over the gathered men, his voice ringing out like the strike of flint against stone. "If we wait, we will only wait to die."

A murmur of agreement rippled through the warriors. Some nodded, others clenched their fists, their jaws tight.

Tobáhá sat motionless, his expression unreadable. He let the words settle before he finally spoke. "War is not a single battle, Nähtöh. It does not end because we spill their blood." His voice was calm, but there was an iron weight beneath it, the kind that only came from years of experience. "You call for war. And then what? The soldiers will not disappear. Their numbers will not shrink because we strike at them in anger."

Nähtöh turned sharply toward him, his face twisting with frustration. "And if we do nothing, what then? Do you think they will stop? Do you think they will look at the bones of our dead and decide they have taken enough?" He scoffed, shaking his head. "You speak as if we have a choice. But we do not. We can fight now, or we can wait for them to kill us in our sleep."

The fire crackled between them, the only sound in the tense silence that followed.

[CHAPTER 6] — BLOOD AND ASHES

Before she could think better of it, Tala stepped forward. Her heart pounded, but her voice did not waver. "If we strike without thought, we will only lose more."

All eyes turned to her. Some, like Tsénatokwa, regarded her with quiet understanding. Others, like Nāhtöh, did not bother to hide their disdain.

"You would have us do nothing?" he asked, his tone sharp.

"No," she answered. "I would have us be smart." She met his glare, refusing to back down. "We cannot win by attacking like a wounded animal, lashing out without thinking. That is how they expect us to fight. That is how they want us to fight. If we move too soon, too recklessly, they will be ready. And they will crush us."

A few warriors exchanged glances, their expressions shifting. Others remained unmoved. One man scoffed under his breath, shaking his head. "What does she know of war?" he muttered. "She carries white blood. Maybe she would rather we bow to them."

The words hit like a slap, but she did not flinch. She lifted her chin. "You say I carry white blood, but I have never lived among them. I know nothing of their kindness— only their cruelty. Do not mistake my caution for weakness." Her gaze swept over the warriors, her voice steady. "We should not let them decide when we fight. We should decide. And we should strike when they least expect it."

A few heads nodded, some hesitant, some firm. One of the older warriors, a man who had seen many battles, grunted in approval. "She speaks sense," he admitted.

[CHAPTER 6] — BLOOD AND ASHES

But Nāhtöh did not look convinced. His dark eyes burned as they locked onto hers. He said nothing, but the weight of his gaze was a challenge in itself. She had not only stood against him—she had questioned him. And he would not forget it.

Tobáhā let the tension stretch before he spoke again. "There is truth in both words," he said at last, his tone measured. "We must fight. But we must fight wisely." His gaze drifted to Tala, then back to the warriors. "I will speak with those who know the land. We will watch the soldiers. Learn their movements. And then we will decide when to strike."

It was not the answer Nāhtöh had wanted. But it was the answer the council had settled on.

One by one, the men stood and walked away, their faces still tight with anger, but the decision had been made. The night stretched on, but the fire burned lower, and soon only embers remained.

Tala lingered a moment longer, her hands clenched at her sides. She could still feel Nāhtöh's glare like heat against her skin. She had made another enemy tonight.

As she turned toward her tipi, the weight of it all settled over her. She closed her eyes, but sleep did not come.

The night smelled of smoke, of decisions made in grief, of war waiting on the horizon. The world she knew was unraveling, and she did not know how to stop it.

[CHAPTER 7] — A STRANGER AMONG THEM

Two days had passed since the last scouting party rode out, and in that time, the camp had gone about its daily rhythms, though an undercurrent of tension remained. The Comanche knew the white men would return, always pushing farther, always wanting more. The scouts had gone to learn where the soldiers moved, to see if the threat crept closer. No one expected their return to come with such a ruckus before the sky had even begun to lighten.

The commotion started as a distant clamor, carried ahead of the warriors by the sharp cries of excitement and fury. Dogs barked, children stirred from their blankets, and women stepped from their tipis, pulling shawls around their shoulders against the night's chill. As the warriors neared, the flickering firelight cast their forms in sharp relief, their voices rough from exhaustion and triumph. At their heels, a limp figure was dragged through the dust, his body leaving a dark smear in the dirt.

More and more of the camp gathered, stepping out from their shelters, some still bleary-eyed, others already gripping weapons in instinct. The man being pulled behind the lead warrior was barely conscious, his head lolling to the side, face streaked with blood. His uniform was unmistakable, tattered and smeared with dirt but still bearing the colors of the U.S. cavalry. The sight of it sent a fresh ripple of rage through the crowd.

[CHAPTER 7] — A STRANGER AMONG THEM

"A soldier," someone spat, the word carrying the weight of years of suffering, of raids, of lost family.

"He's near dead already," another voice called out. "Save him the trouble—cut his throat and be done with it."

The man groaned weakly as the warriors dragged him into the heart of the camp, tossing him onto the packed earth like a carcass stripped of its usefulness. He barely moved; his breath ragged. Deep gashes marred his arms and chest, his lower leg twisted unnaturally. One eye was swollen shut, his lip split and caked with dried blood.

"Look at 'im," an elder sneered. "Ain't even fit to fight. That don't mean he ain't a danger."

"Don't need to fight to bring death," another voice answered. "Maybe he's just the first. Maybe more are comin'."

A few murmured in agreement, the fear of more soldiers lurking just beyond the hills prickling like needles down spines. Others looked at the man's feeble attempts to move, his fingers twitching in the dirt, and scoffed.

"He ain't ridin' nowhere like that," one of the younger warriors said, nudging the man's boot with the butt of his lance. "Ain't got a gun, ain't got a horse. Don't seem much of a threat now."

Tala stood among the growing crowd; her breath steady but her heart pounding against her ribs. She knew how this would go if left unchecked. The Comanche had no patience for their enemies, not when the scars of past betrayals still bled fresh. But this was no battlefield. This was their home,

[CHAPTER 7] — A STRANGER AMONG THEM

and what they did now would mark them, one way or another.

"Kill 'im now," a warrior near the front growled. "Ain't no use keepin' a rattlesnake alive."

"He's worth more than a corpse," another voice countered, older and measured. "Might have information. Might be worth tradin'."

"And might bring more soldiers down on us just by bein' here," the first snapped.

The argument swelled, voices overlapping, tempers sharpening to the edge of violence. Tala saw hands tighten on weapons, saw the shift in the crowd's stance, the readiness for action.

A single hand rose above the din. Tobáhā.

The chief's presence alone carried weight, but his raised palm silenced all. The people turned toward him; their breaths held in check. Tobáhā's gaze swept over the gathered people before settling on the crumpled soldier at their feet.

"The council will decide," he said, his voice firm.

A few dissatisfied murmurs rumbled through the crowd, but none openly defied him. The chief's word was law, and all knew better than to challenge him before witnesses.

Before another word could be spoken, an elder stepped forward, her face lined with the wisdom of many seasons. Tsénatokwa, the camp healer. She crouched beside the unconscious soldier, examining his wounds with the practiced eye of someone who had seen too much suffering.

[CHAPTER 7] — A STRANGER AMONG THEM

"A decision made now is no decision at all," Tsénatokwa said, shaking her head. "He is not long for this world unless tended to. Let him heal, then let him answer for himself."

Some scoffed, others nodded in reluctant agreement. The healer had a voice that few ignored.

Tobáhā turned then, his dark gaze falling directly on Tala. She felt the weight of it settle on her, solid as stone. The fire crackled between them, casting long flickers of gold across the chief's face.

"You will see to his wounds," Tobáhā said, the command clear.

Tala stiffened. The unease that had coiled in her gut tightened. She had expected this, and yet she still felt her stomach twist. The soldier was the enemy. A killer of her people. He wore the uniform of those who had slaughtered families, stolen land, driven the buffalo farther and farther away. And now she was to heal him?

Still, she did not hesitate. Her fingers curled into fists at her sides, but she gave a single nod.

The chief held her gaze for a long moment, then turned away, signaling an end to the discussion. The gathered Comanche slowly began to disperse, though many still threw distrustful glances at the barely-breathing soldier.

Murmurs slithered through the crowd, barely hushed, but sharp enough that Tala felt them like burrs caught in her skin. Some didn't bother to keep their voices low.

[CHAPTER 7] — A STRANGER AMONG THEM

"Why her?" a woman muttered to another, just loud enough for it to carry. "Half-white blood don't make her one of them."

"She speaks their tongue," an older man grunted. "Knows their ways better than most."

"And what's to say she won't take his side?" another voice challenged. "Maybe that's why Tobáhā chose her. If he dies, we say it was her fault."

Tala felt her spine stiffen, though she didn't raise her head. She had heard these things before, her whole life, but hearing them now, with the entire camp watching, made the heat rise in her chest. She was neither fully Comanche nor fully white, a fact that had been decided for her the moment she was born. Now, it marked her as something apart— useful when needed, suspect when not.

She swallowed hard, forcing herself to ignore the whispers, the eyes tracking her every movement. The chief had given an order. She could not refuse.

Drawing in a breath, she took a slow step forward. The soldiers' uniform was tattered, stained with blood and dust, his body lying twisted where the warriors had left him. His face, streaked with grime, was barely visible beneath the bruises. She hesitated just for a moment before kneeling beside him. The dirt was cold beneath her, the scent of sweat, blood, and leather thick in the air.

Her fingers hovered near his forehead before she pressed her palm against his skin. Heat pulsed beneath her touch. Fever. His breath was uneven, his chest rising in shallow bursts, lips cracked and dry. Beneath the filth, she could feel the slick dampness of sweat beading along his

[CHAPTER 7] — A STRANGER AMONG THEM

brow, his body burning up beneath the layers of grime and injury. He was lost in it, somewhere between wakefulness and oblivion.

"He's dyin' already," a voice called from behind her. "Let him finish."

Tala didn't answer. She let her gaze travel over his wounds, assessing. Deep gashes across his chest and arms, not fresh but not yet healing. A wound on his leg, likely from a fall or a bad landing—broken or at least wrenched badly enough to keep him from standing anytime soon. Blood had seeped into the torn fabric of his trousers, and his hands, curled loosely at his sides, bore fresh scrapes. The wounds were harsh, brutal even, but they weren't fatal.

If she tended them, if she gave him water, kept him cool, and let his body fight—he would live.

She wasn't sure if that was the right thing to do.

The boyishness of his face startled her. Beneath the filth and bruising, he wasn't much older than her. Maybe twenty. The sharp lines of his jaw and cheekbones were softened by unconsciousness, his face stripped of whatever hardness it might've held in life. The soldiers she had seen before, those who came to fight, to drive her people from their lands, had been older, hardened, lined with years of bloodshed. This one wasn't like them. Or maybe he was, but the fever had stolen that part away.

A tangle of emotions twisted in her chest—pity, curiosity, resentment.

"Does he deserve it?" She didn't realize she had spoken aloud until she heard the sharp breath of the man beside her.

[CHAPTER 7] — A STRANGER AMONG THEM

Tsénatokwa crouched at her side, her weathered hands resting lightly on her knees as she studied the soldier with the slow patience of an old hunter watching a wounded animal. But there was no malice in her gaze, only a quiet knowing.

"Deserve what?" the healer asked, her voice steady and worn, like a river smoothing stone.

"Mercy."

Tsénatokwa did not answer right away. Her dark eyes, wise and unreadable, flicked to Tala, then back to the soldier. She exhaled slowly, as if weighing the weight of all the lives she had seen lost before this one.

"Deserve don't hold much meaning in times like these," she said at last. "Life don't measure fairness. The river don't stop flowin' for grief, and the wind don't turn back for sorrow. We live because we are given breath, and we die when the time takes it from us. Ain't the spirits decidin' it. Ain't even Tobáhā. Just the way of things."

Tala frowned. "You sayin' it don't matter?"

Tsénatokwa shook her head, her lined face unreadable. "I'm sayin' you already know what you're gonna do." Her voice softened, though the weight of it pressed deep into Tala's bones. "You just need to let yourself do it."

Tala's lips pressed together. She did know.

She stood, brushing the dust from her hands. "He can't stay here," she said, looking at the warriors who still stood nearby, watching. "Move him to the horse pickets. Build a shelter. He's too weak to fight, but if he wakes, he don't need to be among the families."

[CHAPTER 7] — A STRANGER AMONG THEM

One of the warriors snorted. "He won't be wakin' soon."

"Maybe not," she allowed. "But if he does, I want him where I can watch him."

Another voice chimed in, this one more reluctant. "If Tobáhā wants him livin' long enough for the council to decide, he'll need a place to mend."

The agreement was hesitant, but it was there. Within moments, two warriors bent, each gripping one of the soldier's arms, hoisting him up between them like a sack of grain. His head lolled to the side, barely making a sound, too lost in fever to feel much of anything.

Tala followed as they carried him past the main tipis, past the soft glow of the fires where women stirred pots of morning meal, past the younger warriors who were tending to the herd. The air smelled of damp grass, horse sweat, and the rich musk of animals that had settled for the night.

A temporary lean-to was quickly fashioned, poles dug into the earth, thick hides stretched across them. It was simple, meant to keep the wind off his back and give some measure of cover. One of the warriors who had carried him gestured to the ground.

"This is where he'll die," he muttered.

Tala crouched as they lowered the soldier onto a pile of furs, careful not to jostle his leg too much. He barely reacted, save for a faint hitch in his breath.

She stared at him for a long moment.

Not dead. Not yet.

[CHAPTER 7] — A STRANGER AMONG THEM

She reached for her water skin, uncorking it. Tilting his head, she pressed the mouth of the skin against his lips, dribbling only a few drops at a time. At first, there was nothing, but then his throat moved, weakly swallowing. A flicker of something stirred behind his closed eyelids, a twitch of life, but it was fleeting.

Tala then went and gathered what she needed under the watchful gaze of Tsénatokwa, the elder woman's hands moving with quiet precision as she sorted through her stores of dried herbs. She worked without hurry, pressing a bundle of yarrow into Tala's palm before selecting willow bark, her fingers brushing over the rough texture as if listening to something only she could hear. Tala filled a small clay bowl with fresh water from a larger vessel, the cool weight of it settling in her grip as she tucked a strip of clean cloth into her bundle.

"You already know what they'll say," Tsénatokwa murmured, her voice low, steady.

Tala tied the bundle tight, keeping her expression even. "It don't change what I gotta do."

Tsénatokwa let out a soft breath, something between approval and resignation. "No, it don't."

With that, Tala turned, stepping away from the firelight and back toward the lean-to, the supplies held firm in her grasp, the weight of what lay ahead pressing just as heavy.

Tala sat in the dim shelter, the crude lean-to offering little against the chill creeping into the night. The air carried the scent of trampled grass and horses, their occasional snorts and the shifting of hooves filling the quiet spaces between the distant voices of warriors deep in debate. The

[CHAPTER 7] — A STRANGER AMONG THEM

firelight from the main camp barely reached where she knelt, casting only a dull glow over the prone figure before her.

She worked by touch as much as by sight, fingers expertly sorting through the small bundle of herbs and dried roots she had brought with her. The cool edge of a flint knife pressed against her palm as she carefully shaved willow bark into fine curls, gathering them into a clay bowl. She had seen enough fevers to know that if he lived through the night, he might have a chance. If he did not, then Nāhtöh and those like him would not have to argue further over his fate.

The voices of the warriors sharpened, pulling her thoughts toward them despite herself.

"He should die before sunrise," Nāhtöh said, his voice hard as bone. "Wouldn't take much. A knife in the ribs, quick and clean. The white men don't deserve more than that. Think of those we've lost. My cousin, your brother—how many more before we stop takin' pity on 'em?"

Murmurs rippled through the group, some in agreement, others more cautious.

"He's not worth the trouble of killin'," another voice countered. "He's dyin' already. Maybe we let the spirits decide."

"And if he don't die?" Nāhtöh shot back. "Then what? We keep him? Feed him? Patch him up so he can tell his people where to find us?"

Tala reached for a waterskin, blocking out the rising argument. She would do what she had always done—heal. The warriors could debate, the council could decide, but her task was clear.

[CHAPTER 7] — A STRANGER AMONG THEM

She dampened a strip of cloth, wringing out the excess before pressing it gently to the soldier's forehead. His skin burned beneath her touch, fever taking hold.

He stirred. A faint sound, little more than a dry breath escaping his cracked lips. Tala paused, watching as his brow furrowed, his face twisting slightly. His mouth parted, a murmur slipping free—soft, broken, but unmistakable.

She caught it. English. The words blurred together, slurred by fever and exhaustion, but she understood them.

"Don't… don't let me…"

His voice was weak, barely there, but the weight of it settled deep in her chest. The warriors nearby would not understand, nor would they care. He was an enemy, a thing to be decided upon, nothing more.

But in that moment, as she sat beside him, hearing the fractured remnants of whatever thought lay behind his fevered mind, she knew.

His presence here would change everything. For him. For the camp. And for her.

[CHAPTER 8] — THE EDGE OF DEATH

Tala moved with practiced efficiency, her hands swift and sure as she sifted through the bundles of dried herbs hanging from the tipi's ceiling. The scent of crushed sage and juniper clung to the air, mingling with the lingering traces of woodsmoke. Fever was often deadlier than the wound itself—she had seen strong warriors felled not by the blade that cut them, but by the heat that burned them from within. She would not let this man die, not if she could help it.

She unwrapped a bundle of willow bark, breaking it into smaller pieces with nimble fingers before reaching for the pouch of bitter root. The others might question why she wasted her skill on a white soldier, but she didn't care. Right now, he was not a soldier. He was a man caught in the grasp of the sickness that had taken too many before him.

The fire flickered low as she poured fresh water into a clay pot, setting it among the glowing embers. It hissed and spat as the heat worked its way through, sending small wisps of steam curling upward. Tala dropped the willow bark into the bubbling water, adding dried yarrow for strength, slippery elm to soothe, and a pinch of goldenseal to ward off further sickness. The bitter scent filled the air, sharp and pungent.

She scooped the steaming mixture into a hollowed-out gourd, then stood, ducking out of the tipi into the cool night air. The camp was quiet, the fires burning low, their embers pulsing like the heartbeat of the land itself. She moved

[CHAPTER 3] — THE EDGE OF DEATH

toward the lean-to at the camp's edge, where the soldier lay, his body still caught between fever and unconsciousness.

She crouched beside the sleeping man, dipping a hollowed-out gourd into the mixture. The fever had him now, his body trembling beneath the thin buffalo hide that covered him. His breath came in ragged pulls, his skin slick with sweat. She pressed her palm against his forehead—too hot. He wouldn't wake, not yet, but she had to get the medicine down his throat before the sickness took a deeper hold.

Sliding an arm beneath his head, she lifted him just enough to press the gourd to his lips. "Drink," she murmured, though she knew he could not hear her. Carefully, she tilted the vessel, allowing the warm liquid to trickle into his mouth. Some dribbled down his chin, but he swallowed enough to count. Tala let him rest again, brushing damp strands of hair from his forehead.

She worked through the night, wringing out cool cloths and laying them across his skin, trying to pull the fever from him. She pressed them to his brow, his neck, his chest, replacing them as soon as the heat warmed them beyond use.

Outside, she could hear the warriors passing by, their moccasins whispering against the packed earth. She knew they were watching. She could feel their eyes on her, some filled with suspicion, others with quiet condemnation.

"She should let the sickness take him," a voice muttered from the dark, just beyond the lean-to.

Another scoffed. "She wastes her skill on a snake."

[CHAPTER 8] — THE EDGE OF DEATH

Tala didn't turn, didn't acknowledge them. It didn't matter what they thought. She had been an outsider in her own way for as long as she could remember. Half Comanche, half something else, belonging everywhere and nowhere at once. If they had words for her, let them speak them outside. Inside the lean-to, this man's survival was hers to fight for.

The days passed in a blur of heat and restless sleep. She worked in near silence, tending to him, her own exhaustion pulling at her limbs. Each morning she checked his wound, unwrapping the bandages to inspect the deep cut along his side. The bleeding had stopped, and the edges of the wound were beginning to knit together, but the fever was unrelenting.

At night, he tossed and turned, muttering in the white man's tongue. But it was not the sharp, commanding voice she had heard from men like him before. It was softer, confused, lost in a world of dreams. His brow furrowed, his lips forming words she barely caught.

Once, in the stillness of night, his hand clenched the blanket beneath him, his breath coming fast. "Don't... leave," he murmured, the words strained, heavy with longing.

Tala frowned. She had seen men lost in fever dreams before, but there was something different in his tone. She leaned closer, her fingers brushing against his forehead as she adjusted the cloth.

"Who?" she asked, though she knew he could not answer her.

[CHAPTER 8] — THE EDGE OF DEATH

His expression twisted as if searching for something just beyond reach. Then, in a hushed, desperate voice, he whispered a name she did not recognize. It was not a name of his people. Not a Comanche name.

Tala sat back on her heels, watching him as he drifted further into whatever world his fever had trapped him in. Whoever he was calling for, it was not her. But the way he spoke, the way the name fell from his lips, made something tighten in her chest.

She did not know this man's story. But she would keep him alive long enough to tell it.

The following evening, the sky stretched wide above the camp, streaked with the last remnants of daylight. The deep blue of the encroaching night swallowed the sun's lingering hues, the stars beginning to pierce through like scattered embers. A fire burned at the center of the gathering, its glow casting flickering shapes across the seated men.

Tala stood near the edge of the gathering, the warmth of the flames reaching toward her but not quite touching. She kept her arms folded over her chest, her expression unreadable as she listened to the voices around her.

"He has not woken," one of the warriors said, his gaze sharp as he stared at the fire, as if the answer lay within the embers. "He takes up food. Water. And for what? He is a soldier, and soldiers bring death."

Several heads nodded in agreement. The council had been patient, more than some had wanted, but that patience was wearing thin.

[CHAPTER 8] — THE EDGE OF DEATH

"Healing takes time," Tsénatokwa said, her voice steady, the weight of years pressing into her words. "The body does not rise when it is called. It rises when it is ready."

"And if it does not rise?" the first man pressed, eyes narrowing.

Tala watched the elder's face. Tsénatokwa rarely gave more words than necessary, and that was what made the warriors listen to her. She did not rush to speak, did not let her tongue wander where it need not go.

"If he does not wake, then he will not trouble us," Tsénatokwa said simply.

"That is not an answer."

A man Tala recognized well—Nokoni, a fierce warrior whose brother had been cut down by soldiers not long ago—stepped closer to the fire. His stance was tense, his jaw set. "We should not wait to see if he wakes. We should not wait for him to heal. A clean death now is better than giving him the chance to bring death to us later."

Another man, seated with his arms resting on his knees, exhaled sharply. "He would not be the first to come riding against us once his wounds are gone."

A murmur of agreement rippled through the gathering. Tala felt the weight of their distrust pressing into her, though none of them looked at her directly. It was not her decision to make, but they all knew she was the one standing between the man and death.

"If we let him live," Nokoni continued, voice low, "it is only a matter of time before he repays us with steel."

Tsénatokwa studied the fire. "Perhaps."

[CHAPTER 8] — THE EDGE OF DEATH

"Perhaps is not good enough." Nokoni's voice tightened, his fingers curling into fists. "You know what the soldiers do. What they have done. What they will keep doing. You think he is different?"

Tsénatokwa lifted her head then, her dark eyes meeting Nokoni's. "I think he is one man. Not an army."

Nokoni's nostrils flared, but he said nothing.

Tala forced her hands to remain still at her sides, though she could feel her own pulse in her fingers. They were waiting for someone to say it outright, for the decision to be made. Too many wanted him dead, and few, if any, would protest it.

She turned her gaze toward the tipi where the man lay, his body still caught between life and whatever else lay waiting for him.

She should not care. He was just another wounded man, another patient. She had tended to warriors before, both Comanche and others, and she had done her duty without giving them a second thought once they were well enough to leave. But this one was different.

She could not forget the way his fevered voice had carried something she could not name, something deeper than pain. She had heard suffering in the voices of dying men before, had heard fear and anger and sorrow. But his words had been full of something else.

Regret.

That unsettled her more than anything.

The night deepened as the discussion went on, but the argument had not changed. The warriors who wanted him

[CHAPTER 8] — THE EDGE OF DEATH

dead still wanted him dead, and the few who spoke for patience had no real ground to stand on.

Tala remained at the edge of the gathering, her face unreadable. She knew she should walk away, that this was not her fight, not her place to decide.

But when Tsénatokwa's voice broke through the thick silence once more, it was not to end the matter.

"Let us wait until he recovers, giving him more respect than his kind would give us."

Nokoni exhaled sharply, clearly frustrated. But even he would not openly defy Tsénatokwa in front of the council.

"We will wait. But then we will decide," the elder finished.

The men began to rise, the meeting breaking apart. Some moved toward their tipis, others to their horses, but Tala did not linger among them. She turned and walked away, her feet carrying her back toward the lean-to where the man lay.

She stood outside for a long moment, listening to the quiet of the night. The camp had settled, only the occasional murmur of voices and the distant snort of a horse breaking the stillness. The fire's glow cast long, flickering shapes across the ground, and beyond that, the land stretched into darkness, open and vast beneath the endless sky.

Tala exhaled, stepping inside the lean-to. The air was thick with the scent of earth, dried herbs, and the lingering traces of sweat and blood. The man lay still, his breath steady but shallow, his chest rising and falling in the slow rhythm of deep sleep. His body no longer burned with fever,

[CHAPTER 8] — THE EDGE OF DEATH

but the sickness had left him weak, his skin drawn and pale beneath the bruises.

She crouched beside him, her fingers hovering just above his forehead before she let them rest there, feeling for warmth. Cool now. He was through the worst of it. And yet, he did not wake.

She studied him in the dim light, searching for something in his features that might explain why this man, out of all those who had come against her people, had survived. His uniform, torn and stained with dirt and blood, still marked him as the enemy. And yet, stripped of his strength, with no weapon in his hand, he did not look like a soldier now.

Just a man caught between two worlds.

Returning to her tipi, sleep came for her quickly that night, pulling her into the depths of her own mind.

She was at the river again.

The water was cold around her ankles, clear and rushing, spilling over smooth stones worn by time. The sky stretched wide above her, painted in deep blues and streaks of red, the last gasps of a setting sun. The wind carried the scent of rain, though no storm yet touched the land.

She turned, her gaze sweeping across the riverbank.

Her mother stood there.

Not as she had been in her final days, when sickness had drained the life from her bones, but as Tala remembered from childhood—strong, upright, her dark hair falling down her back in a thick braid. She did not smile, did not speak, but her eyes held something Tala could not place.

[CHAPTER 8] — THE EDGE OF DEATH

Tala stepped forward, her feet sinking into the damp earth. "Mother?"

The word carried, but her mother did not answer. Instead, she lifted her arm, pointing upstream, toward where the water bent around the trees, vanishing from sight.

Tala followed her gaze.

The river was changing.

The current, once steady, twisted in upon itself, rippling in strange, unnatural patterns. The colors in the water deepened, darkening, turning to hues she had never seen in water before. A sound, low and distant, rumbled from beyond the bend, something she could not name but felt in the pit of her stomach.

She turned back to her mother, but she was no longer there.

The river swelled, rising higher, the wind carrying it upward in curling tendrils, reaching toward her, wrapping around her legs like grasping hands. She tried to move, but the water pulled her in deeper, stealing the ground from beneath her feet.

A voice—her mother's voice—finally reached her, though it did not come from where she had stood. It came from the water, from the wind, from everywhere and nowhere at once.

"Change is coming."

Tala fought against the pull, her breath catching as the water surged higher, wrapping around her waist, her chest, her throat.

[CHAPTER 8] — THE EDGE OF DEATH

Tala woke with a sharp inhale, the tipi around her still and silent. Her skin was damp with sweat, her pulse a hammer in her chest. The dream clung to her, its weight heavy, the sensation of water dragging her under still lingering in her limbs.

She pushed the buffalo hide covering aside and sat up, brushing a hand over her face. The fire outside had burned low, the embers barely casting enough light to reach the edges of the tipi. The distant sounds of the camp settling for the night reached her ears—soft murmurs, the shifting of horses, the occasional crackle of firewood.

But her thoughts were not on the camp. They were on the man.

The council's impatience, the river's unnatural churn, the way her mother had stood at the water's edge pointing toward something unseen—everything tangled together in her mind. She exhaled slowly, grounding herself in the cool night air, but it did little to push the unease away.

She needed to see him.

Rising, she pulled a shawl around her shoulders and stepped outside, the evening breeze brushing against her skin. The sky stretched wide, clear and dark, the stars scattered thick across it. The lean-to where he lay was on the far edge of the camp, not far from the horses, where he would be easy to keep an eye on.

Her feet moved soundlessly over the earth as she made her way toward him. The lean-to was little more than a crude shelter of branches and hide, enough to shield him from the wind but not enough to offer real comfort. He was still an

[CHAPTER 8] — THE EDGE OF DEATH

outsider, still unwelcome to most, and no one had any desire to make him feel otherwise.

Tala crouched beside him, studying his face in the dim light. He was still as before, his chest rising and falling in slow, measured breaths. He looked less like a soldier now—less like a threat.

She reached out, fingers grazing his forehead. Cooler now. The fever had broken, but still he had not woken.

She should have felt relief.

Instead, she only felt the weight of the dream pressing against her ribs.

Tala dipped the cloth into the cool water, wrung it out, and pressed it to his forehead. The fever had passed, but his body remained weak, his breaths shallow. She had seen many men fight sickness before, had watched warriors claw their way back from the brink of death with sheer will alone. This man had no such fire in him—not yet.

She studied his face in the dim light. He was unshaven, his features drawn tight from the strain of his body's battle. His hair was damp, sticking to his forehead, the curls lighter than those of the men she had grown up with. Even in sleep, there was something restless about him, as if his body was aware of the danger even when his mind was lost in fevered dreams.

As she reached for a fresh cloth, his breathing hitched. A slight twitch in his fingers, a shift in his chest—then, his eyelids fluttered, the movement faint at first, almost imperceptible.

Then, they opened.

[CHAPTER 8] — THE EDGE OF DEATH

Tala froze, her hand hovering over the bowl of water. His eyes were blue, startlingly so, like the sky after a hard rain. They were dulled with sickness, clouded from exhaustion, but even in his weakened state, there was something sharp behind them.

For a long moment, he simply stared at her.

She did not move. Did not speak.

The fire crackled outside, the distant murmur of the camp just beyond the lean-to, but here, inside this small space, there was nothing but the silence stretching between them.

Then, panic flickered across his face.

His chest rose too quickly, his breath catching as though he might bolt upright, but his body refused him. His limbs trembled, weak from the days spent unconscious, his muscles betraying whatever his instincts screamed at him to do. His fingers flexed against the thin blanket, gripping the fabric as if he might use it to steady himself.

Tala remained still; her expression unreadable. She had seen many wounded men wake, had witnessed the moment their minds caught up with their bodies. Some woke with anger, some with fear. This one woke with both.

His cracked lips parted. "Where am I?"

The words came hoarse, nearly broken, as though his throat had been scraped raw. He barely got them out, his breath thin, his voice a whisper of what it should have been.

Tala's breath caught.

No one else in this camp would understand those words. No one else could answer him.

[CHAPTER 8] — THE EDGE OF DEATH

Her fingers curled around the damp cloth in her lap. English had been her father's tongue; the language he had spoken to her in quiet moments before he disappeared. He had taught her words, phrases, the rhythm of it, though she had not understood why it mattered then. After he was gone, her mother had continued the lessons, long after there was any reason to. The language had always felt like something separate from her, something that belonged to another life. But here, now, it pressed against her like a weight.

She hesitated.

If she spoke his tongue, if she revealed she understood him, it would make her position in the camp all the more precarious. Many already questioned her place, already eyed her with suspicion for tending to him. If they knew she was talking to him, knew she could grant him understanding where they could not, it would not go unnoticed.

But the man was looking at her now, waiting. His breathing was uneven, his body still shaking from exhaustion, but his mind was grasping for something solid, something to anchor him.

Slowly, she forced herself to answer.

"You are in my camp."

Her voice was measured, her English careful, the words rolling off her tongue in a way that still felt foreign, though she had spoken them before.

The blue of his eyes darkened with realization.

She saw it, the way it settled in him, the way the truth took hold. His body may have been too weak to fight, but

[CHAPTER 8] — THE EDGE OF DEATH

his mind had just caught up. He knew where he was now. He knew what that meant.

And she knew, in that moment, that the true battle had only just begun.

[CHAPTER 9] — BETWEEN HOSTILITY AND HEALING

Harrison Grant's eyelids fluttered, heavy as lead, the world around him shifting in and out of focus like the dim, flickering lamplight of a distant saloon. His body felt weighted, pinned down by exhaustion and something far worse—pain, deep and relentless, wrapping around him like a noose. He sucked in a slow, ragged breath, but even that small effort sent a fresh jolt of fire through his ribs.

His mind clawed through layers of fog, grasping at memories that refused to come together in any sensible way. The last thing he remembered clearly was the taste of dust in his mouth, the sharp snap of gunfire—no, not gunfire, something else, something harder to place. Then there had been movement, jolting, harsh, hands gripping him, dragging him, and voices that blurred into one indistinct hum.

Now, he was here. Wherever *here* was.

The air smelled different—earthy, rich with the scent of leather, fire, and something bitter, medicinal. His vision swam, shifting between vague outlines and sudden clarity, and he became aware of the rough texture beneath him, something not quite a cot, not quite the ground. The walls above him were not walls at all, but stretched hide, shifting slightly with the air. A lean-to, built sturdy but temporary. Not a fort. Not a cavalry outpost.

[CHAPTER 9] — BETWEEN HOSTILITY AND HEALING

He tried to move, tried to push himself up even an inch, but his body refused him, a searing pain exploding along his ribs, stealing what little breath he had. A groan rumbled in his throat, unbidden, weakness bleeding into his bones. His mouth was dry as sand, his tongue thick and useless against the roof of his mouth.

A woman sat nearby; her presence quiet, watchful. She did not startle at his sound, did not shift or lean forward with concern. She simply studied him, her gaze unreadable. Even through the haze dulling his thoughts, he recognized that she was Comanche. Her long dark hair was pulled back loosely, her face still and patient. Her clothes, the beaded deerskin, the fringed edges, the bone jewelry at her wrists, all confirmed what his sluggish mind had already guessed.

His breath came heavier now, his body tensing, though he was in no shape to fight. He had heard stories, all of them grim. Men taken from battlefields only to be finished off later, or left to die slow, painful deaths. He tried to push himself up again, but his strength betrayed him, his limbs shaking, his ribs protesting the effort.

Harrison's breath hitched, confusion warring with the pain still clawing at his side. She had spoken his language. That meant she *understood* him. That meant... what?

His thoughts jumbled together, but one thing remained clear—he needed water.

He parted his lips, tried to form the word, but his throat barely cooperated. "Water," he croaked, the request nearly lost in the effort it took to force it out.

She didn't hesitate this time. Reaching beside her, she lifted a wooden bowl filled nearly to the brim. The scent of

[CHAPTER 9] — BETWEEN HOSTILITY AND HEALING

damp earth and soaked bark clung to the liquid inside, and he knew it wasn't just water, but something else, something meant to keep him alive.

She brought the bowl toward him, shifting slightly so she could support his head. But as she moved closer, he reacted without thinking, his body working on instinct alone. His fingers shot forward, closing around her wrist.

Her skin was warm beneath his touch, her pulse steady. His grip was weak, too weak to hold her for more than a moment, but he didn't let go right away. It wasn't an act of defiance, nor a challenge. He didn't even know why he did it. It was as though he needed to ground himself in something, *someone*, to remind himself that he was still alive, still *real*.

Her expression flickered—not quite surprise, not quite anger. Just the barest trace of something unreadable before it disappeared again.

She didn't pull away.

Instead, she adjusted her grip, helping him as she brought the bowl to his lips.

The first sip burned its way down his throat, rough from days without water. But it was good. He drank slowly, careful not to choke, the warmth of the liquid spreading through him, waking up something inside him that had nearly gone cold.

Even as he drank, his eyes never left hers.

She was not afraid of him. Not wary in the way one might be of a wounded animal, nor gentle in the way a healer

[CHAPTER 9] — BETWEEN HOSTILITY AND HEALING

might tend to the dying. She simply watched, quiet, unreadable, waiting.

He swallowed, the last of the liquid settling in his stomach, and for the first time since waking, he wondered if survival was truly what he should want.

Tala sat back; her dark eyes steady as she studied the man before her. His breathing had settled somewhat, though his chest still rose and fell with the slow, careful rhythm of someone in pain. The water had helped, but his body was still weak, his wounds still raw. He was too pale, his skin drawn tight over his cheekbones, his lips cracked despite the drink she had given him. He would live—perhaps—but it would not be an easy road.

She let out a slow breath, then spoke in his language, her voice even. "How did you come to be wounded?"

His gaze flickered with something unreadable. His Adam's apple bobbed as he swallowed, his throat still raw from thirst. He hesitated, his brow knitting together as if he had to drag the memory forward from some deep, dark place. For a long moment, she thought he might not answer.

Then, his voice, rough and uneven, broke the silence.

"My unit was ambushed." he rasped, pausing as if to test whether his words would come at all. He licked his lips, his gaze drifting for a moment before settling back on her. "We was ridin' west, meant to regroup with another detachment, but we never made it. One minute, we're clear, the next—" He exhaled, shaking his head slightly. "Arrows rained down like a damn storm, horses panicked. I remember shootin', but I don't remember hittin' anything. Just ridin', fast as I could, tryin' to keep my head down.

[CHAPTER 9] — BETWEEN HOSTILITY AND HEALING

Then there was a jolt, like the whole damn world tipped sideways, and I was fallin'."

His fingers twitched where they lay against the thin blanket, as if reliving the moment. "Must've landed bad. I remember the pain, splittin' through my leg. Horse was gone. The rest—" He inhaled sharply, his gaze unfocused for a moment before he looked at her again. "Rest is just bits and pieces. Some yellin'. Hooves thunderin' past. Then nothin'."

Tala did not speak right away, absorbing his words, watching him carefully. The world outside the lean-to was still, but not silent. The fire crackled, distant voices murmured beyond the camp. She could feel the weight of the air pressing in around them.

A shift of movement caught her attention, and the flap of the lean-to rustled as a figure stepped inside.

Nokoni.

The warrior's dark eyes flicked between them, assessing. He did not speak, nor did he need to. Suspicion settled in the air like smoke. He did not linger long—just long enough for his gaze to settle on Tala, sharp as flint, before he turned and stepped back outside.

Tala let out a slow breath, her body tense in a way that had nothing to do with the man lying before her. She knew well enough what Nokoni had been thinking. What they all were thinking.

Every interaction with this soldier was being watched. Judged. Weighed against her already fragile standing.

[CHAPTER 9] — BETWEEN HOSTILITY AND HEALING

She turned her focus back to the wounded man, watching as he tried to shift, pushing against the earth in a feeble attempt to sit up. He barely lifted himself an inch before pain struck, his muscles locking up, a ragged groan breaking past his clenched teeth.

His body was too weak, too battered to follow his mind's urgency. He collapsed back onto the makeshift bedding, his breath ragged, sweat breaking out along his brow.

Tala tilted her head, her voice barely more than a murmur, almost to herself. "You should not be alive."

A flicker of something passed through his tired eyes—something sharp, edged with a humor that did not reach his lips.

"And yet, here I am," he said, his voice dry with exhaustion.

Tala did not reply. Instead, she reached for his bandages, fingers working deftly as she began to unwrap the cloth at his side. The wound was healing, but slowly. The edges were no longer raw, but they still bore the deep marks of infection, the skin bruised and mottled.

Her fingers brushed against his ribs, just lightly, and his breath hitched.

She paused, her dark gaze flicking to his face.

Something passed between them in that moment. An awareness. A realization that neither of them could put into words.

Neither of them spoke.

[CHAPTER 9] — BETWEEN HOSTILITY AND HEALING

Tala exhaled through her nose and continued her work, though her own pulse was not as steady as it had been before.

That night, the fire burned low in the center of the camp, the flames curling around blackened logs, sending thin trails of smoke into the night air. The gathered men sat in a circle, their faces lit in flickering orange, their expressions grave. Tala stood just beyond the firelight, her arms crossed, her body still as she listened. She was not part of this council, not meant to have a voice in this matter, but she knew the weight of this night. It would shape what happened next, not only for the soldier but for her as well.

Nāhtöh, as she expected, was again the first to speak. His voice carried with the force of someone who had already decided the outcome. "Letting him live is an insult," he said, his dark eyes sweeping over those seated around him. "How many of ours have they taken? How many children have been left without fathers? How many women without sons?" His hand curled into a fist against his knee. "A soldier is a soldier, whether he carries a weapon or not. He did not ride alone. He was with others, others who came to kill us. If we spare him, what does that say of us?"

A few of the younger warriors nodded, their faces tight with anger, but others were less certain. Tala watched Tobáhā from where she stood, his features unreadable as he rested his elbows against his knees, staring into the fire. When he finally spoke, his voice was calm but firm. "It is not honor to kill a man who cannot defend himself."

Nāhtöh scoffed. "And is it honor to let him live? To let him return to his people and bring more death to our doorstep?"

[CHAPTER 9] — BETWEEN HOSTILITY AND HEALING

Tobáhá did not react to the challenge. He took his time, letting the silence stretch between them before answering. "If he dies here, it changes nothing. The soldiers will still come. They will not know his fate, and they will not care." He shifted, glancing toward the lean-to where the soldier lay. "But if he lives, we may learn something from him. What he knows, where his people are, how many ride."

Nāhtöh's jaw tightened. "You think he will tell us anything we do not know?"

Tobáhá met his gaze. "You think he will not?"

A murmur ran through the gathered men, some considering, others still unconvinced. Tala could feel the tension in the air, thick as the smoke rising into the night sky.

She knew that if she spoke now, if she offered even a single word in the soldier's defense, she would pay for it. The looks, the murmurs, the way some already eyed her with suspicion—it would only grow worse. She had spent her whole life proving herself, being more than what they accused her of being. And yet, she knew what she would do before the thought even fully formed in her mind.

She turned, stepping away from the fire before she could give herself a chance to change her mind. The decision was not yet made, but she had heard enough to know that the battle over the soldier's life was not yet lost.

As she approached the lean-to, the night stretched around her, cool against her skin. The voices of the council faded behind her, replaced by the crackle of distant fires, the low murmur of men speaking in hushed tones. She pulled

[CHAPTER 9] — BETWEEN HOSTILITY AND HEALING

back the flap of the lean-to, stepping inside, her eyes adjusting to the dimness within.

The first thing she saw was his eyes.

He was awake.

Not just stirring, not just caught between sleep and wakefulness, but fully aware, watching her with an intensity that sent something cold curling through her stomach.

He said nothing at first, his gaze steady, his expression unreadable. The fever was gone from his eyes now, leaving only sharp clarity in its wake. There was no fear there, no expectation of kindness. Only waiting.

Tala exhaled, feeling the weight of the night pressing into her. He did not ask if he would live. He already knew that decision was not hers to make.

[CHAPTER 10] — THE GREAT DIVIDE

The days passed in a slow, tense rhythm. Each morning, Tala checked his wounds, changed his bandages, forced bitter medicine past his lips when he resisted. He still struggled to sit up for more than a few moments at a time, but his strength was returning, slow and stubborn as a drought-weary stream finding its way back to life.

And with that strength came his sharp tongue.

She had known it would. The fever had kept him quiet, too weak to protest much beyond a few mumbled words, but now that he was clearer, he had found his voice.

"This ain't right," he muttered as she pressed a damp cloth to his ribs, wiping away the remnants of dried blood. "Ain't right to keep a man like this, sittin' here, waitin'."

She didn't answer.

"How long you gonna keep me here?" he pressed, tilting his head against the makeshift bedding to get a better look at her. His blue eyes had lost the fevered glaze, and now they pinned her with something sharper. "You speak my tongue, so I know you understand me."

She wrung out the cloth in a bowl of cool water, silent.

His jaw tightened. "You don't have a say, is that it?"

She ignored him, reaching for a fresh strip of linen.

"You gotta have some idea," he said, voice thick with frustration. "You tellin' me you don't know what they mean to do with me? Or you just won't say it?"

[CHAPTER 10] — THE GREAT DIVIDE

Tala pressed the bandage against his wound a little harder than necessary. He sucked in a sharp breath, biting back whatever curse had been forming on his tongue. She could feel his irritation rising, pressing between them like the heat of the sun on dry earth.

His voice dropped lower, quieter. "They mean to kill me, don't they?"

She hesitated. Not because she didn't know the answer, but because she wasn't sure he needed to hear it. Not yet.

"Your fate ain't mine to decide," she said finally, keeping her voice steady.

He exhaled through his nose, turning his gaze to the lean-to's ceiling as if looking for answers there. "That's what I figured."

The silence stretched between them. The fire outside crackled, men's voices carrying in low, indistinct tones from the camp beyond. A horse snorted somewhere nearby, its hooves shifting in the packed dirt.

"Don't like not knowin'," Harrison muttered after a while.

"Most don't."

He huffed a quiet laugh, humorless. "Ain't no way to live."

Tala tied off the bandage with careful fingers, smoothing it against his skin. "And yet, you still do."

His gaze snapped back to her at that, something unreadable flickering in his expression.

For a moment, neither of them spoke.

[CHAPTER 10] — THE GREAT DIVIDE

The next day, he asked again. And the day after that. The frustration between them built like storm clouds over the prairie, thick and restless. He hated not knowing, hated feeling helpless. She could see it in the way he clenched his fists when she ignored his questions, in the way his jaw tightened when she gave him nothing.

"Who decides?" he asked on the fourth day, his voice edged with impatience.

"Tobáhā and the council."

"And what's they waitin' on?"

Tala pulled the bowl of fresh water closer, dipping a cloth into it. "The council speaks. Some want you dead. Some want to trade you. Some wait to see what use you might be."

Harrison let out a dry chuckle. "Some debate over whether I'd make a better corpse or a better bargain."

She said nothing.

He ran a hand over his face, fingers scraping against the stubble along his jaw. "They ever keep men like me alive?"

"This is the first time."

"That ain't much comfort."

"It wasn't meant to be."

His lips pressed into a thin line. She could see the fight in him, the part of him that wanted to stand, to run, to take back control of his fate. But his body wouldn't let him, and neither would she.

Finally, he let out a slow breath, tilting his head toward her. "What about you?"

[CHAPTER 10] — THE GREAT DIVIDE

She frowned. "What about me?"

"You're different from the rest of 'em. You speak like me. Ain't never met a Comanche that spoke English like you do."

She focused on wringing out the cloth, avoiding his gaze. "I learned."

"That ain't an answer."

"It's the only one you're gettin'."

His lips quirked, the faintest hint of a smirk. "So, I ain't the only one bein' kept in the dark."

She sighed, shaking her head, before tilting the gourd to his lips. He drank this time without protest, though she saw the flicker of irritation in his eyes. He hated needing her help, hated the way his body still betrayed him.

"If you want to ask questions, answer some first," she said.

He snorted. "That how this works? A trade?"

She shrugged. "You want control over somethin'? Start there. Tell me about how you became a soldier."

Harrison Grant let out a slow breath, his gaze drifting toward the sloped ceiling of the lean-to, as if the story he was about to tell was written somewhere above him. When he finally spoke, his voice carried the weight of years that had passed too quickly, of choices that had shaped him long before he had ever set foot on this land.

"I was born in Kentucky," he said, his words careful at first, as if choosing them one at a time. "Near the Green River, in a place that don't much matter to anyone who don't come from there. My folks had land—not much of it, but

[CHAPTER 10] — THE GREAT DIVIDE

enough. Grew tobacco mostly, ran a few cattle, planted what we could to get by. Wasn't easy livin', but we made do."

His voice shifted, softened just slightly, taking on the weight of memory. "Had two older brothers, Nathan and Thomas. Nathan was the strong one, the one meant to take over the farm someday. Thomas—" He exhaled slowly. "Thomas was always more like me. He had that itch, that restless feeling, like maybe there was somethin' bigger out there beyond the fields and the riverbanks."

Tala listened without speaking, absorbing the pieces of his past as he laid them before her.

"My ma, she was the steady one. Held us together when times got lean. She was the kind to sing while she worked. Always had some old tune hummin' under her breath, some song her mother taught her, I reckon. Said it helped pass the time, helped the work go by easier. She used to tell me I had a restless soul, that I was always lookin' beyond the hills, always wantin' to see more than what was in front of me. My pa—" A humorless chuckle left him. "Pa didn't believe in soft words or easy days. He expected us to work from sunup to sundown, no complaints, no foolin' around. Said a man's worth was measured in the sweat on his brow, not in the nonsense he got caught dreamin' up."

Tala understood men like that. She had seen them in her own people—those who thought duty and tradition were the only things that mattered, that dreaming of something beyond was a waste of time.

"First time I ran away, I was twelve," he admitted, almost to himself. "Didn't make it far. Got caught sleepin' in a barn 'bout ten miles out. Old fella who owned the place

[CHAPTER 10] — THE GREAT DIVIDE

whipped me good, then sent me right back home. Pa whipped me again for good measure. Figured that'd cure me of wantin' to leave. It didn't."

A dry chuckle, void of humor. He shifted slightly, wincing as the movement sent pain lancing through his side.

"I was fifteen the next time I thought about leavin' for good," he admitted. "Didn't know where I'd go, just knew I didn't want to be tied to that land forever. My pa, he had other plans. Wanted me to be like Nathan, to help run things when the time came. But I weren't made for it. Tried to tell him once—told him I didn't see myself spendin' my whole life in one place, tillin' the same dirt, raisin' the same cattle. He didn't take kindly to that. Said I had my head full of foolishness."

His jaw tightened slightly. "The thing about foolishness, though... sometimes it gets in your blood, and once it's there, ain't no getting it out."

Tala studied him, watching the tension in his face, the way his fingers absently curled against the blanket.

"About ten years ago, when I was sixteen, a man came ridin' through town. Wore his belt loose, pistols on his hips, ridin' a horse that looked like it had carried him across half the country. Said he was headin' west, lookin' for men willin' to ride. Didn't say much about what kind of work it was, but I didn't care. West was better than stayin' put. So I left."

He let out a slow breath, as if still seeing that day in his mind. "Didn't get far before I learned the world don't much care about boys lookin' for adventure. Ended up workin' cattle for near couple of years, driftin' from one ranch to the

[CHAPTER 13] — THE GREAT DIVIDE

next. Hard work, good pay if you didn't mind bein' saddle sore and covered in dust. But that itch in me never settled. Seemed like no matter where I was, I was always wantin' to be somewhere else."

Tala tilted her head slightly. "So why the cavalry?"

Harrison's lips pressed into a thin line. "Ain't many choices for a man who don't own land and don't got a trade. The army was payin' good for men who could ride, and I already knew my way around a horse. Seemed like an easy choice."

She studied him for a moment, considering. "You went from one battle to another."

He let out a dry chuckle, though there was no humor in it. "Ain't that the way of things?"

Tala had seen it before—men like Nāhtöh—men who only knew how to fight, who had no place in a world without war. But she wasn't sure if that was who he was, or if he was just a man who had never figured out where he belonged.

"And now?" she asked.

His gaze met hers, something unreadable flickering behind his tired blue eyes. "Now, I'm lyin' here, wonderin' if all that runnin' was worth it."

Tala said nothing, but something in his words sat heavy in her chest. He had chosen his road, just as she had chosen hers. She wondered if either of them had truly had a choice at all.

Silence settled between them. She let his words hang, waiting to see if he'd offer more. He didn't.

[CHAPTER 10] — THE GREAT DIVIDE

Instead, he turned his attention back to her. "Now it's your turn."

She frowned.

"How'd you learn English?" he asked, his voice lighter but no less curious. "Ain't many of your people who speak it, not like you do."

Tala hesitated.

"My father was white. He taught me," she said finally.

She saw the understanding flicker across his face, the pieces slotting into place.

He didn't press further; didn't ask the questions others might have. Instead, he simply nodded, settling back against the bedding, as if that answer was enough.

Later that evening, Tala worked in silence outside the lean-to, her hands steady as she ground the dried herbs into a fine powder. The rhythmic scrape of stone against stone filled the small space, a familiar sound that had always soothed her, yet tonight, she felt restless. The flickering firelight cast long shapes across the walls, stretching and shifting as the flames danced in the low evening breeze. The scent of crushed bark and dried flowers thickened the air, mingling with the lingering smell of sweat and old blood.

She knew he was watching her.

She did not have to look to confirm it. The weight of his gaze pressed against her skin like a tangible thing, steady, unrelenting. Not the wary, guarded look of a man waiting for a knife in the dark, nor the calculating stare of a soldier trying to size up a new enemy. It was something

[CHAPTER 10] — THE GREAT DIVIDE

else—something that made her grip tighten slightly on the pestle.

Harrison had propped himself up slightly, his back against the crude bedding of furs and woven mats, his hands resting loosely in his lap. His face was drawn, exhaustion still clinging to his features, but his blue eyes were sharp, clear in a way they had not been before.

She focused on her work, forcing herself to ignore him. She had been stared at her whole life, judged for what she was and what she was not. It should not unsettle her now. And yet, it did.

The silence stretched between them, long and taut, until he finally broke it.

"I don't know if I should be grateful or afraid of you," he murmured, his voice rough but steady.

Her hands faltered just slightly, the motion of grinding pausing for the briefest moment before she forced herself to continue. She had not expected him to speak. Had not expected those particular words.

Something about them struck her deeper than they should have.

She let the silence hang, refusing to look at him. "That you are alive should tell you enough," she said evenly.

His breath was slow, measured. "I reckon it should."

He was still watching her, still waiting for something she did not want to give. She could feel it in the air between them, in the way he did not press but did not turn away either.

[CHAPTER 10] — THE GREAT DIVIDE

Tala finally set the mortar aside, brushing her hands against her skirts to rid them of the lingering dust of crushed herbs. She turned slightly, not enough to face him fully, but enough to see him in her peripheral vision.

His expression had changed. The sharpness was still there, the caution of a man who had spent his life fighting, but there was something else now, something quieter, more searching.

She turned away before he could see the small, bitter smile that pulled at the corner of her lips.

The distant fire of the men crackled, its flames licking hungrily at the stacked wood, sending thin ribbons of smoke curling into the night air. Around it, men sat sharpening their weapons, their hands steady, their eyes hard with intent. Some spoke in hushed tones, their words short, clipped, edged with a quiet fury that needed no embellishment. Others said nothing at all, their focus entirely on the gleaming blades in their laps, on the spears they tested between calloused fingers. The tension in the camp had thickened with each passing day, coiling like a snake waiting to strike.

Tala could hear them from where she sat, just outside the lean-to, her hands resting on her knees, her breath slow and steady. She was not part of their circle, but she felt their anger, felt the weight of it pressing against her even from a distance. They had been patient, some more than others, but patience had its limits. Soon, a decision would have to be made, and she knew well enough that the longer the soldier lived, the harder it would be to justify his presence.

She was standing between two sides.

[CHAPTER 10] — THE GREAT DIVIDE

She had always known it, had felt it since she was a child, since the first time another girl had sneered at her, since the first time a warrior had looked past her as though she were something less, something uncertain. Her mother's blood had given her a place among them, but her father's had left her standing at the edge of the circle, never quite inside.

And now, with this man's life in her hands, she saw it more clearly than ever.

To the warriors sharpening their knives, she was a complication. She had not just saved a man they saw as an enemy—she had forced them to wait. Forced them to consider. And that was a dangerous thing. When the answer was clear, when vengeance burned hot in the blood, hesitation was its own kind of betrayal.

And yet, she knew, in the eyes of the white men, she would never be one of them either. If the soldier left this place, if he rode back to his own people and she went with him, what would they see when they looked at her? Not a woman who had saved a life. Not a healer. Just another savage girl who had once belonged to the enemy.

She hated that Harrison's presence forced her to acknowledge the truth—she had never fully belonged to her people.

The realization settled inside her like a stone in her chest, cold and heavy. It should not have hurt; she had known it all her life. And yet, sitting here, with the fire in the distance and the man inside the lean-to still breathing because of her hands, it cut deeper than she had expected.

[CHAPTER 10] — THE GREAT DIVIDE

Returning to her tipi, the night stretched long. Sleep did not come easily.

She lay beneath her buffalo hide, listening to the wind move through the camp, to the distant murmur of voices, to the occasional snort of a restless horse. She shifted, staring up at the stretched hide above her, at the faint patterns of soot that clung to its surface from the fires that had burned through the seasons.

She had made a choice.

And it might cost her more than she realized.

The weight of it pressed against her, but she did not turn away from it. She had spent too many years watching, waiting, hoping to find the place where she truly fit. But she would not let that uncertainty dictate her now.

She exhaled slowly, pressing her eyes shut.

She did not regret saving him.

And that, perhaps, was the most dangerous truth of all.

[CHAPTER 11] — THE TIES THAT BIND

The wind carried a sharp bite through the camp, slipping through the seams of tipis and tugging at the fringes of deerskin garments. It was not yet the dead of winter, but the warning was there, crisp and undeniable. Soon, the snows would come, the rivers would slow beneath layers of ice, and the land would harden beneath the weight of the cold.

Tala stood just outside the lean-to, arms crossed, her dark eyes scanning the sky. The seasons had their own rhythms, their own rules. The time for preparation was growing thin. If Harrison had any hope of surviving, he could not afford to remain weak much longer.

She turned back inside, where he sat, legs stretched before him, his frame still gaunt from the fever that had nearly taken him. He was improving, but too slowly. The time for rest was over.

She reached for his arm. "Come," she said, her tone leaving no room for argument.

Harrison frowned, his blue eyes flicking up to meet hers. "Come where?"

"Up."

He gave a huff of something that might have been amusement or exasperation. "You sure about that?"

[CHAPTER 11] — THE TIES THAT BIND

She didn't answer. Instead, she pulled at his arm, forcing him to shift. He gritted his teeth as he braced his palms against the ground, his muscles shaking with the effort.

Pain carved its way across his face, but he didn't let it stop him. He lifted himself an inch, then another, his breath coming sharp and uneven. Tala said nothing, only waited.

He managed to get one knee beneath him, then the other, his weight trembling on his arms as he pushed himself upright. His legs were unsteady, the strain visible in every fiber of his body.

His jaw tightened. "Ain't this a bit soon?"

"You wish to lie here all winter?"

Harrison let out a slow breath. "Not particularly."

"Then stand."

He let out a curse under his breath, but he did as she commanded. His legs wobbled, the strength not yet returned, but he forced himself to straighten. His hands curled into fists at his sides as he fought against the weakness still clinging to him.

For a moment, it looked as if he might collapse, but he held on, breathing hard through clenched teeth.

Tala watched; her face unreadable. "Again."

Harrison shot her a look, part annoyance, part exhaustion. "Damn woman, let me catch my breath."

She only raised a brow.

With another muttered curse, he tried again. This time, he did not falter as much. The shaking in his limbs was still

[CHAPTER 11] — THE TIES THAT BIND

there, but his body was beginning to remember itself, beginning to obey him once more.

He took a breath. Then another. Then, gritting his teeth, he took a step.

It was small, unsteady, but it was a step.

Tala nodded in approval. "Again."

He gave her a glare, but he did not stop. He took another step, then another. His boots scuffed against the packed earth, his breath coming in hard exhales, but he did not fall.

The effort was painted across his face—pain, exhaustion, determination all battling for space. But then, something else flickered in his expression.

Pride.

It was small, just a sliver of something he had likely long forgotten, but it was there. He turned his head toward her, a grin breaking across his face, breathless but triumphant. "I guess I ain't dyin' yet."

Despite herself, despite every reason not to, Tala felt a smile tug at the corner of her lips. She should not have let it show, but in that moment, she did not stop herself.

The moment her smile broke free; a storm gathered on the horizon.

Nokoni's voice struck like a blade through the crisp evening air, his anger cutting through the quiet. The heavy thud of his footsteps sent a ripple of unease through the camp as he stormed toward them. His dark eyes blazed with betrayal; his face twisted in something deeper than mere fury. It was disappointment, raw and biting, and it was aimed squarely at Tala.

[CHAPTER 11] — THE TIES THAT BIND

"You show kindness to the enemy," he spat, his voice sharp as flint, carrying enough weight to still the air around them.

Tala turned to face him fully, refusing to flinch, though she could feel the shift in the camp. The people nearby had gone still, their hands hovering near their blades. The wind carried the scent of smoldering wood and tanned hides, but it did nothing to mask the tension crackling between them. Nokoni stood rigid, every muscle in his body coiled tight, as if barely holding himself back.

Harrison stiffened beside her. For the first time since he had awakened, she saw it—a flicker of true fear in his eyes. Not the kind born from weakness, but the kind of man who had survived enough to know when his life hung by a thread.

Tala squared her shoulders, refusing to let the weight of Nokoni's fury press her down. She met his glare with one of her own, her voice steady despite the fire in his eyes. "I do what I was taught and told to do," she said evenly. "To heal."

The silence that followed was thick, suffocating. Nokoni's nostrils flared, his fists clenching at his sides. His chest rose and fell with the force of his breathing, but he did not strike, though she could see in the rigid line of his body that he wanted to. His fury was barely contained, teetering on the edge of violence.

"You shame your blood," he growled. "A warrior's strength is in knowing when to show mercy and when to strike." He jerked his chin toward Harrison, his lip curling in disgust. "You waste your hands on a snake."

[CHAPTER 11] — THE TIES THAT BIND

Tala held his gaze, unyielding. "A man is not a snake just because you name him one."

His eyes darkened, and for a moment, she thought he might raise his hand, that his fury might finally boil over. But he only exhaled sharply, his jaw tightening until she thought his teeth might crack beneath the pressure. Then, with a stiff jerk of his head, he turned on his heel and strode away, his anger trailing after him like smoke in the wind.

Tala let out a slow breath, feeling the weight of the moment settle deep in her chest. People gathered nearby watched her, some with curiosity, others with barely veiled judgment. She had crossed a line, even if she hadn't meant to. Nokoni's words had not been a warning—he had already decided what she was in his eyes. And now, so had the others.

Beside her, Harrison shifted slightly, his movements slow, still careful from the weight of his injuries. His voice was quiet but firm. "You didn't have to do that."

Tala turned her head slightly, catching the way his brows pulled together, confusion threading through the exhaustion in his face. He had not understood the words exchanged between her and Nokoni, not the language itself. But he had understood everything else. The tension. The anger. The way Nokoni had stood like a blade ready to strike, and the way Tala had not backed down.

Harrison wasn't a fool. He had spent enough time in dangerous places, around dangerous men, to know when someone wanted him dead. And he had seen the moment pass between them—the fire in Nokoni's stance, the sharp

[CHAPTER 11] — THE TIES THAT BIND

edges of his fury, and the judgment that had settled on Tala like a weight she might never shake off.

Tala exhaled, the air leaving her lungs slower than she meant it to. She kept her gaze ahead, fixed on the horizon beyond the camp, but her words were for him. "Yes, I did."

She could feel his eyes on her, studying her in that way he did, as if he was trying to piece together a puzzle with too many missing parts. But he did not press her for an answer, did not ask why she had chosen to put herself between him and a man who might have gladly spilled his blood on the dirt.

She did not know if she could have answered him even if he had. But deep down, a sliver of doubt crept in, an uneasy whisper beneath her ribs. Had she just made a mistake that could not be undone?

That evening, the fire outside the lean-to crackled low, sending the scent of burning cedar curling through the night air. Tala sat with her knees drawn up, arms wrapped around them, watching the embers shift and stir like restless spirits. The camp had begun to quiet, but tension still clung to the air like a coming storm.

She knew she was being watched before she heard the footsteps. The soft brush of moccasins against the earth, the measured pace—there was only one person in the camp who moved like that, with the slow patience of someone who had seen too many seasons to be rushed by any of them.

Tsénatokwa lowered herself to the ground beside Tala, her joints creaking slightly with the motion. The old healer did not speak at first, letting the silence settle between them.

[CHAPTER 11] — THE TIES THAT BIND

Tala kept her eyes on the fire, waiting, knowing the words were coming.

"You walk a dangerous path," Tsénatokwa said finally, her voice quiet but firm. "One that will only lead to sorrow."

Tala's jaw tightened. She felt the words settle in her chest, heavy as stones. She had known this was coming. The stares, the murmurs when she passed, the way Nokoni had not been the only one who looked at her with anger tonight.

She had chosen this.

Still, she did not argue. She could not. Tsénatokwa was right.

"I know," Tala said at last, the words barely more than a breath.

Tsénatokwa studied her, her expression unreadable in the firelight. "Then why do you do it?"

Tala turned her gaze upward, toward the vast stretch of sky above them. The stars were scattered thick and bright, as they always were in these open lands, untouched by the smoke of the white man's cities. They had watched over this land long before she was born and would continue long after she was gone.

She could not put the answer into words. She did not know how to explain the way she felt when she had pressed that damp cloth to Harrison's fevered brow, when she had listened to the weight in his voice as he spoke of his past, when she had seen something in his eyes that did not belong to a man who deserved to die.

The truth was, she did not regret saving him. Even now, with her people doubting her, with warriors sharpening their

[CHAPTER 11] — THE TIES THAT BIND

knives in anger, she could not bring herself to wish she had let him die.

Tsénatokwa sighed, her fingers tightening briefly around the medicine pouch at her waist. "There are things that cannot be undone, Tala. You know this."

Tala nodded. "I know."

The old woman was silent for a long moment, then she reached out, fingers brushing lightly over Tala's arm—an unexpected gesture, more comfort than warning. "Do not lose yourself in this, child," she murmured. "Do not forget who you are."

Tala did not answer. She wasn't sure she knew anymore.

Tsénatokwa lingered only a moment longer before rising to her feet, her figure outlined against the fire's dying glow. She did not say anything else as she turned and walked back toward her own tipi, vanishing into the darkness of the camp.

Tala sat still, her hands tightening into fists against her legs.

She knew the truth in Tsénatokwa's words. She had seen the way the warriors looked at her tonight, the way her people were beginning to question where her loyalty lay.

And yet, she could not bring herself to regret what she had done.

The night was deep and quiet, the fire outside the lean-to burning low, casting only a soft flickering glow across the packed dirt. Tala sat just beyond its reach, knees drawn up, arms wrapped around them as she gazed out at the stillness

[CHAPTER 11] — THE TIES THAT BIND

of the camp. The warriors had settled into uneasy rest, though she knew many remained awake, their minds too full of battle and vengeance to allow sleep to claim them.

Harrison sat across from her, his back to the rough frame of the lean-to, hands held close to the fire's warmth. His movements were slow, still burdened with the weight of healing, but he no longer looked like a man clinging to life. He looked like a man trying to understand where he stood.

His fingers flexed, rubbing warmth into his palms, his gaze fixed on the flames as if searching for something there. He had not spoken in a while, but she could tell his thoughts were restless. Tala watched him, studying the lines of his face, the set of his jaw, the way his shoulders tensed and relaxed as though he carried some burden that had not yet left him. He did not look like a prisoner. Not anymore.

She exhaled softly, tilting her head upward. The sky stretched wide and endless, filled with stars so thick they seemed to press down upon the earth itself. They had always been there, watching, unmoved by the blood spilled beneath them, indifferent to the war between their peoples. Time did not shift for men's battles. It did not pause for grief or hesitation. The stars had seen warriors rise and fall, land stolen and reclaimed, and they would continue shining long after all of them were gone.

Harrison shifted slightly, the quiet rustle of fabric against earth pulling her attention back to him. He did not look at her, but she knew he was aware of her watching. His face was unreadable, but there was something in his expression, something in the way his gaze flickered between the fire and the darkness beyond it, that made her wonder.

[CHAPTER 11] — THE TIES THAT BIND

For the first time, Tala questioned whether they were both searching for the same thing.

She should go. She should return to her tipi, let the night settle, and let the space between them remain exactly that—space. But she did not move. She could not. Something held her in place, some unseen tether, fragile yet unyielding.

She was too aware of the quiet between them. It was not the silence of enemies, nor the indifference of strangers. It was something else entirely, something unspoken but heavy, something neither of them had the words for.

Harrison turned his head slightly, finally looking at her. His blue eyes reflected the firelight, filled with the same quiet unrest she felt in her own chest. He did not speak, but he did not need to. The weight of this moment stretched between them, neither of them willing to break it.

The wind stirred through the trees, carrying a breath of cool air across the camp, rustling the dry grass and sending a ripple through the fire's glow. Tala shivered, but it was not from the chill. It was from the realization settling deep in her bones.

She had already crossed a threshold she could never return from.

Even as she told herself that this was dangerous, that she was standing too close to something she could not control, she did not look away. She did not move. And for the first time, she did not know if she wanted to.

[CHAPTER 12] — BENEATH THE PAINTED SKY

Harrison took another slow step forward, his breath measured, his body still stiff from weeks of recovery. The ground beneath him was solid, packed from years of use, but his legs felt uncertain, as if they had forgotten what it meant to bear his weight. Tala walked ahead, her pace steady but unhurried, not offering him a hand, not looking back to see if he kept up, but aware of him all the same.

The camp stretched wide before them, alive with movement. The air carried the scent of woodsmoke, drying hides, and cooking meat, mingling together in something distinctly familiar yet entirely foreign to him. Voices rose and fell in a steady rhythm—women speaking as they worked, children laughing as they darted between tipis, warriors sharpening weapons and tending to their horses.

Harrison's gaze swept over it all, drawn in by the sheer energy of the place. He had spent enough time fighting against men like these, yet he had never truly seen them. Not like this.

A woman crouched beside a wooden frame, her hands working swiftly as she stretched a deerskin taut, scraping it clean with smooth, practiced strokes. Nearby, another woman knelt over a shallow pit, carefully turning thick strips of bison meat on a drying rack, the smoke from the smoldering embers beneath curling around her in lazy tendrils. Children ran past them, weaving between the workers with unbridled energy, their laughter ringing through the crisp autumn air. Some of the younger ones held wooden sticks, pretending to hunt one another, while an older boy practiced drawing back the sinew string of a small bow, his face scrunched in concentration as an elder adjusted his grip.

Harrison had never seen a place so full of life, so woven together by the hands of its people. This was not the kind of thing the army talked about when they spoke of the Comanche. They spoke of raids, of warriors, of wild, untamed men on horseback who rode like the wind and vanished just as quick. But this—this was not a gathering of savages. This was something more.

This was a home.

He watched as an older man sat cross-legged in front of a group of boys, his voice low but steady, his hands moving expressively as he spoke. The children were still, hanging on to his every word. A few feet away, another elder traced symbols into the dirt with a smooth stone, a young girl watching closely, her small hands mimicking his movements as she tried to follow. These were lessons, stories, knowledge passed down not through books or preachers or schoolhouses, but through the lips of those who had lived it.

A short distance away, warriors gathered in a loose circle, their voices quiet but firm as they inspected arrows, tightening sinew and sharpening stone tips. Horses stood nearby, tethered loosely, their ears flicking at the sound of voices, their breath rising in the cool morning air.

[CHAPTER 12] — BENEATH THE PAINTED SKY

Harrison let out a slow breath. He had grown up on a farm, a place where every hand had a purpose, where survival meant working together. But this—this was something deeper. The efficiency, the quiet rhythm of it all, the way each person seemed to fit into the whole—it was unlike anything he had seen before.

And yet, he felt the weight of their eyes on him.

Warriors, women, even the elders—many had paused in their tasks, their gazes following him as he moved through the camp. Some held open suspicion, others merely a detached wariness, but all of them were watching.

He was a soldier, an enemy. He was a reminder of the world that pushed in from the outside, the world that had already brought war to their doorstep more times than he could count. He knew he did not belong here, and they knew it too.

But as he walked, as he saw the way they worked, the way they spoke, the way they prepared for the harsh months ahead, he found himself wondering how much of what he had been told had been a lie.

Tala walked ahead, her dark braid swaying gently against her back, her shoulders squared but relaxed. She did not look at him, but she didn't have to. She knew he was watching. She knew he was seeing something he had never seen before.

And though she would never ask it, though she would never speak the question aloud, he felt it in the space between them.

Do you understand now?

[CHAPTER 12] — BENEATH THE PAINTED SKY

Harrison inhaled deeply, the crisp air filling his lungs.

Yes, he thought.

He understood.

A couple of nights later, as the last traces of daylight stretched across the sky, Tala led Harrison away from the camp, her steps steady but unhurried. He followed without question, though he cast a glance back at the flickering campfires, the distant murmur of voices fading as they walked further into the open land.

The air was crisp, carrying the scent of earth and the faintest traces of smoke. They moved beyond the outer edges of the tipis, past where the horses were tethered, and toward a ridge that sloped gently upward. The land stretched wide before them, untamed and vast, rolling hills and sweeping plains reaching toward the horizon.

Harrison took a steadying breath, his gaze sharpening as he took in the sight. The sky above them was painted in hues of orange and violet, the last embers of daylight giving way to deepening blue. Stars had begun to pierce through, scattered like grains of salt across the heavens, shimmering in the endless expanse. It was the kind of sight that a man could lose himself in, something so grand and endless that it made his own existence feel impossibly small.

Tala stopped at the crest of the ridge, lowering herself to sit on a flat stretch of earth. She pulled her legs beneath her, resting her hands lightly on her knees. Harrison hesitated for a moment before lowering himself beside her, though he kept a bit of distance between them, uncertain if his presence here was truly welcome.

[CHAPTER 12] — BENEATH THE PAINTED SKY

For a long while, neither of them spoke. The world around them felt too large for words, the quiet settling between them like a living thing, breathing in the spaces they did not fill.

Then, at last, Tala broke the silence.

"My mother used to bring outside the camp to places like this," she said, her voice softer than he'd ever heard it. "When I was a child, she would take me to the high places, the quiet places, and tell me to listen."

Harrison turned his head slightly, watching her in the dimming light. "Listen for what?"

She lifted her chin slightly, gazing out over the land as the wind stirred the grass in slow, rhythmic waves. "For the stories the land tells," she murmured. "The way the wind moves through the plains. The way the grass bends and shifts. The sky, the rivers, the way the earth cracks and dries in the summer, then softens in the spring." Her fingers brushed absently against the ground. "She said that if you listen, truly listen, the land speaks."

Harrison watched her closely, something in her words settling deep in his chest. "And what does it say?"

Tala exhaled, a faint trace of something unreadable crossing her face. "That nothing ever truly belongs to anyone." She turned her gaze to him then, her dark eyes steady. "The land does not belong to the people. The people belong to the land. It gives, and it takes, and it does not care who claims it."

Harrison let out a slow breath, letting her words sink in. He had spent his life surrounded by men who believed land

[CHAPTER 12] — BENEATH THE PAINTED SKY

was something to be taken, something to be owned. It was measured, sold, fought over. Men had killed for it. Governments had drawn lines on maps, cutting through it as if it were something that could be contained.

But sitting here, looking out over this vast, untamed stretch of land, he understood what she meant. This place had been here long before the white men had named it, long before the first fence had been hammered into the earth. And it would be here long after.

Tala's gaze drifted back toward the horizon. "Esihabi used to say that the sky tells you everything you need to know, if you know how to read it. She could look at the way the clouds moved and tell if it would rain or if the sun would burn the land dry. She knew when the wind would bring a storm, when the animals would move, when the seasons would shift." Her voice grew quieter, laced with something heavier. "She said the land carries our footprints for only a little while, then washes them away like the river does."

Harrison studied her in the dim light. "She sounds like she was a wise woman."

Tala's lips pressed together, and she gave a small nod. "She was."

There was something beneath those words, something unspoken but heavy. A loss, a grief that she did not give voice to. Harrison had seen that look before, in men who had watched their families die, in those who carried wounds no doctor could mend. He had learned long ago that some griefs were not meant to be pried open.

So, he simply sat beside her, letting the silence return, letting the night settle around them.

[CHAPTER 12] — BENEATH THE PAINTED SKY

Harrison leaned back on his hands, his gaze lifting toward the vast stretch of sky above them. The stars had multiplied in the darkness, spread thick across the heavens in a dizzying sprawl. The silence between them was not uncomfortable, but something unspoken hung in the air, something that had not been there before.

After a long moment, he let out a slow breath. "My mother taught me the constellations," he said, his voice quieter now, touched with something distant. "She'd take me out at night when I was just a boy, sit me down in the grass, and point up at the sky. Said a man should always know how to find his way, no matter where he ends up."

Tala turned her head slightly, watching him in the dim glow of the stars. There was something different in his tone, something softer. "And did you listen?"

He let out a short breath that wasn't quite a chuckle. "When I felt like it," he admitted. "I was young, full of foolishness, always runnin' off, gettin' into trouble. But she had a way of makin' me sit still when she wanted me to. She'd grab hold of my ear, drag me outside, and tell me, 'You ain't gonna be a boy forever, Harrison. Someday you'll have to find your own way home.'"

Tala's lips pressed together, not quite a smile, but something close. "She sounds like she was strong."

Harrison nodded; his gaze still fixed upward. "She was. She had this way about her, never raised her voice much, never needed to. She grew up in the mountains, not far from where I was born. Said her pa used the stars like a map, could tell exactly where he was by how they sat in the sky. She wanted me to learn the same."

[CHAPTER 12] — BENEATH THE PAINTED SKY

He lifted a hand, tracing an invisible line between the stars, pointing toward a cluster twinkling high above them. "There. See that one? The three bright stars in a row? That's Orion's Belt. My mother used to say that if I ever got lost, I should find Orion. Follow the belt west, and it'd lead me home." His fingers shifted, trailing toward another set of stars. "And there's the North Star. Brightest one in the sky this time of year. If you follow it, you'll always know which way is north."

Tala tilted her head slightly, following the lines he drew in the air. She had never thought much about the stars beyond their presence in the sky, never sought meaning in them beyond what was woven into the stories of her people. But as she listened to him, she could hear the weight of memory in his voice, the way his words carried pieces of a past he no longer had.

Harrison dropped his hand back to his lap, his expression unreadable. "I always figured I'd teach my own son someday," he murmured. "Sit him down in the grass, tell him the same things she told me. But I never stayed anywhere long enough for that to happen." He shook his head slightly, exhaling. "War don't leave much room for things like that."

Tala studied him, the way the light played against his features, the way his expression shifted between nostalgia and something heavier, something lost. In that moment, he did not look like a soldier. He looked like a man searching for something he had yet to find.

She glanced back toward the sky, letting her own thoughts drift. "My mother used to say the stars are like the

133

[CHAPTER 12] — BENEATH THE PAINTED SKY

land," she said. "Always there, even when you can't see them. And if you know how to read them, they'll tell you where you need to go."

Harrison looked at her then, his gaze steady, something unreadable passing between them. "Maybe she was right," he said.

The space between them felt smaller now, the quiet no longer filled with hesitation but something else, something fragile and unspoken. Their eyes met, and she felt it—a pull, as if something unseen was drawing them closer, as if the lines between them were blurring in a way that could not be undone.

Harrison shifted slightly, his body tilting toward hers, not in a way that was deliberate but instinctive, something natural. Tala's breath caught, her fingers twitching at her sides, torn between stepping forward and stepping away.

The air around them had changed, the world shrinking down to this moment, to the stars above and the space between them that was beginning to fray.

Suddenly, a sound carried over the ridge, deep and steady, like the heartbeat of the land itself. Tala felt it in her bones before she fully registered what it was, the rhythmic pounding traveling through the earth beneath them.

Drums.

Not war drums. There was no urgency, no sharp tempo meant to summon warriors to arms. This was something older, something sacred. The steady, deliberate beats signaled a ceremony taking place in the camp below,

[CHAPTER 12] — BENEATH THE PAINTED SKY

perhaps a prayer for strength as winter approached, or a song to honor the spirits of those who had walked before them.

But it was enough to break the moment.

Harrison blinked, as if the sound had startled him back to reality. The warmth in his expression cooled slightly, his posture shifting, shoulders tensing as he turned his gaze toward the distant campfires flickering below. He wasn't one of them, and he never would be. Whatever had passed between them—whatever understanding, whatever unspoken thing had hovered between them beneath the night sky—was gone as quickly as it had come.

Tala felt it slip away, like a thread she hadn't realized she'd been holding onto until it unraveled in her hands.

She stood abruptly, brushing dust from her palms. "We should go back."

Harrison hesitated before nodding, his gaze lingering on her for a moment longer than it should have. But he said nothing. He pushed himself to his feet, slower than her, his movements still carrying the stiffness of recovery. His balance wavered, but he caught himself, exhaling sharply as he rolled his shoulders.

The drums continued, their steady rhythm echoing through the valley below, filling the silence between them.

Tala started down the ridge, her steps sure, but her chest felt tight, as if she had been running when she hadn't moved at all. She focused on the path ahead, not looking back, knowing if she did, she might see something in his face she wasn't ready to acknowledge.

135

[CHAPTER 12] — BENEATH THE PAINTED SKY

Behind her, she heard Harrison follow, his boots scuffing against the dry earth.

Neither of them spoke as they made their way back to camp.

[CHAPTER 13] — TREADING DANGEROUS GROUND

The next morning, the rising sun cast long golden streaks across the plains, its light stretching over the quiet camp as warriors returned from their scouting. Tala felt the shift in the air before she heard the murmurs ripple through the people. Something had changed. Something was coming.

By the time the council gathered in the center of the camp, a low tension already weighed over them like an approaching storm. The warriors who had returned stood near Tobáhā's tipi, their expressions grim, their silence heavier than words. Tala kept to the edge, her arms folded, watching. She had seen this gathering before, heard the arguments, but this time, something felt different. This time, patience had grown thin.

A scout stepped forward, his face lined with dust and fatigue. "More soldiers," he reported, his voice firm but quiet. "They ride closer. They search the riverbanks, the hills. They are looking for something. Or someone."

A murmur spread through the assembled men. Some shifted where they sat, others gripped the handles of their knives tighter, eyes darting toward one another. Everyone knew what it meant.

"They are looking for him," another warrior said, glancing toward Tobáhā. "And if they do not find him, they will keep coming."

[CHAPTER 13] — TREADING DANGEROUS GROUND

Nähtöh stepped forward, his jaw set. "Then we make sure they do not find him."

His meaning was clear. His words sliced through the space between them, heavy and sharp. Some of the younger warriors nodded in agreement. Others said nothing, but their silence spoke for them.

Tobáhā remained still, watching. His face gave nothing away.

"Kill him before they come looking," Nähtöh continued, his voice like flint striking stone. "Before the white men send more of their kind. Before they decide we are hiding something. You think they will not come? They will. And when they do, they will not ask questions. They will burn, and they will kill, and they will drag our women away like cattle."

A few men muttered in agreement, their eyes dark and heavy with old memories. There was no forgiveness in those faces. No mercy.

"He is already here," one of the older warriors said, his voice slow but edged with warning. "Killing him now will not change what has already happened. The white men do not need an excuse to come for our land. They take whether we fight or whether we do not."

Nähtöh scoffed, his nostrils flaring. "You say that now, but when they come with guns and fire, you will wish we had not let this snake live."

A different voice spoke, cutting through the growing anger. "And what will we do, Nähtöh? Send his body back to them? You think that will stop their coming?" It was

138

[CHAPTER 13] — TREADING DANGEROUS GROUND

Tsénatokwa. The healer sat cross-legged near the fire, her hands resting on her knees, her gaze calm but unshaken. "You would spill blood here, but it will not stop them from spilling more out there."

Tobáhā finally lifted his chin, the weight of leadership settling heavier on him than on any other man in the gathering. "You are not wrong, Nāhtöh," he said after a long silence. "The white men will come." His dark eyes swept the assembled warriors. "They always come."

There was no disputing that.

Tala shifted where she stood, her hands tightening into fists at her sides. She had no place in this debate, but the words cut through her just the same. She had known this would come, but it was different hearing it spoken aloud. She knew that Harrison was running out of time.

"Then do not wait," one of the younger warriors spoke, his voice filled with a desperate kind of certainty. "We cannot fight an entire army, but we can take one step ahead of them. We move the camp. Leave him behind with nothing. Let the soldiers find what is left of him."

Tala's breath caught. That was worse than simply killing him. It would be condemning him to slow suffering. But she said nothing. Not yet.

Tobáhā did not answer right away, his expression unreadable. She saw his gaze drift toward her for the briefest moment, but he did not hold it. She didn't know what that meant. She didn't know if he had already decided.

The argument continued around her, voices rising and falling, frustration growing. The fear of what the soldiers

[CHAPTER 13] — TREADING DANGEROUS GROUND

would do if they came looking was spreading fast, like dry grass catching flame.

Tala remained still, watching, but inside, something twisted tight in her chest. She had feared for herself many times in her life. She had known what it was to be on the outside, to be watched with suspicion, to feel the weight of doubt pressing down on her shoulders.

But this was different.

This was fear for someone else.

This was knowing that no matter what she had done to keep Harrison alive, no matter what words she might say, she could not stop what was coming.

Tala left the council fire with a tightness in her chest that would not ease. The air in camp had thickened with unease, every warrior and elder knowing that decisions had been made in the heat of anger but not yet spoken aloud. The soldiers would come—that much was certain. The only question now was whether they would be met with an offering of blood or left to find nothing but emptiness. She had listened to every word, every threat, every warning, and yet she had remained still, powerless to shape what was coming.

As she stepped away from the gathering, she let out a slow breath and made her way toward the lean-to. She had expected the weight in her limbs to pull her down the moment she reached her small space, expected the exhaustion to claim her, but when she lifted the flap of the lean-to, it was empty. The blanket where Harrison had been resting was rumpled, pushed aside, but he was not there.

[CHAPTER 13] — TREADING DANGEROUS GROUND

Tala's stomach tightened.

She turned sharply, her gaze sweeping the camp, searching for any sign of him. Then she spotted movement near the horses. A lone figure, moving with careful, deliberate steps.

Harrison.

He was standing beside a horse, attempting to tighten the saddle's cinch, his fingers fumbling as he struggled against the leather straps. He was slow, his body betraying his effort with every motion, but still, he worked with quiet determination, his jaw clenched, his shoulders stiff.

Tala remained where she was for a moment, watching. She half expected him to give up, for his body to fail him before his will did. She thought that perhaps he would realize the futility of what he was doing before she had to intervene.

But then, as he tried to lift himself enough to reach the saddle's stirrup, his knee buckled. His breath hitched, and he caught himself against the horse's side, gripping the leather for support. The animal shifted, unsettled by his unsteady movements.

That was enough.

Tala moved forward, closing the distance between them in a few quick strides. Without a word, she reached for the reins, pulling them from his shaking grasp.

"You are not yet strong enough," she said, her voice even but firm. "You'd fall before you reached the river."

He let out a heavy breath, his body sagging against the saddle. He did not argue, did not bristle at her interference.

[CHAPTER 13] — TREADING DANGEROUS GROUND

Instead, he leaned forward slightly, resting more of his weight against the saddle's side, his fingers curling around the worn leather.

For a long moment, neither of them spoke.

Then, without lifting his head, he said quietly, "Would you stop me?"

The words carried something more than just the question. There was something in them that dug beneath the surface, something raw, something uncertain.

His blue eyes lifted to meet hers, and for the first time since she had pulled him back from the edge of death, she saw something in them that she could not name. A challenge, yes. A quiet defiance. But beneath that, something else.

Tala did not answer right away. Because she did not know the answer.

If he had been stronger, if he had been well enough to truly try, would she have stopped him? Would she have stood in his way, knowing that letting him go might keep the peace in the camp but might also lead to his death?

She held his gaze, searching for something in him that might make the answer clear. But there was nothing. Only questions, ones she was not ready to face.

So, she said nothing.

And the silence between them stretched, long and uncertain, before finally, she looked away.

That night, the fire burned low in front of the lean-to, its flames licking lazily at the dry wood, sending up thin tendrils of smoke that drifted into the night air. The camp

[CHAPTER 13] — TREADING DANGEROUS GROUND

around them hummed with restless energy—warriors murmuring in small clusters, sharpening blades, tending to horses that would carry them into whatever battle lay ahead. The weight of uncertainty pressed over the entire camp, thick as the coming winter, and yet, in front of the fire, there was a pocket of quiet.

Tala sat with her arms loosely draped over her knees, her gaze fixed on the embers glowing beneath the flames. Across from her, Harrison sat with his back against the rough support of a wooden post, legs stretched out, hands resting loosely on his thighs. He had said little since their tense exchange at the horses, and she had offered nothing in return.

She wasn't sure what there was to say.

The firelight cast shifting patterns across his face, deepening the hollows beneath his cheekbones, accentuating the lines of exhaustion that still clung to him despite his regained strength. His blue eyes were distant, focused on something she could not see, his jaw set in quiet contemplation. He looked like a man caught between two fates, neither offering a clear path forward.

She exhaled slowly and finally broke the silence.

"Come inside before they decide to kill you sooner," she said, her tone unreadable.

Harrison's gaze lifted to her, lingering as if weighing her words for more than their surface meaning. He studied her, searching for something she wasn't sure even she could name. For a long moment, he did not move, did not speak. Then, finally, he nodded.

[CHAPTER 13] — TREADING DANGEROUS GROUND

She rose first, brushing the dust from her hands, and turned toward the lean-to. She heard him shift behind her, pushing himself upright, his steps slow but steady as he followed. When she lifted the flap, she glanced back, watching as he hesitated just before crossing the threshold.

"Don't make me regret this," she murmured.

His lips curved slightly, but there was no humor in the expression. "I reckon we both got regrets enough."

She didn't respond, only stepped inside and let him follow.

The air within the lean-to was thick with the lingering scents of dried herbs, earth, and the faint musk of animal hides. It was not a comfortable place—built for necessity, not rest—but it had kept him alive, had shielded him from the eyes that would rather see him dead. She gestured to the bedding she had arranged earlier, the worn blankets still rumpled from where he had lain before.

Harrison lowered himself with care, wincing slightly as his muscles protested the movement. She watched him, waiting to see if he would refuse help, if his pride would outweigh his exhaustion. He settled with a slow exhale, rolling his shoulders against the makeshift bedding before looking up at her.

"You ain't gotta keep doin' this," he said quietly.

She arched a brow. "Doin' what?"

"Lookin' after me. I know what they think. You ain't blind to it neither."

Her jaw tightened, but she did not look away. "I do what I must."

[CHAPTER 13] — TREADING DANGEROUS GROUND

His lips parted, as if he had more to say, but whatever it was, he swallowed it back. Instead, he shifted, settling deeper into the bedding.

She turned away, reaching for the clay pot near the fire. The embers still held enough heat, and she had steeped another brew earlier in the evening—willow bark, yarrow, a pinch of bitter root. The fever was gone, but his body was still recovering. She poured the tea into a small wooden bowl and turned back to find him watching her again.

There was something different in his gaze now, something she did not want to name.

She pushed the bowl into his hands, her fingers brushing his for the briefest moment before she pulled away.

"Drink," she ordered.

He smirked, a flicker of his usual defiance. "You always this bossy?"

"When men are too stubborn to help themselves."

His chuckle was rough, barely more than a breath, but he lifted the bowl and took a slow sip. He grimaced at the taste, but he drank without complaint. When he lowered it, he met her gaze again.

"Why are you really doin' this?" he asked.

Tala didn't answer right away. She wasn't sure she could.

She turned back toward the entrance, listening to the distant voices outside. The warriors were still awake, still planning, still speaking of war. The tension in the camp would only grow stronger in the days to come. The decision

[CHAPTER 13] — TREADING DANGEROUS GROUND

to let him live was being worn thin, stretched to its breaking point. She knew that her protection could only last so long.

She inhaled deeply before speaking, keeping her voice low.

"Because there's more to this world than just killin' and dyin'," she said. "And if you can't see that, then there's nothin' I can do to help you."

She stepped away then, moving toward her own small space, knowing sleep would not come easy.

Behind her, Harrison remained silent, but she could still feel the weight of his gaze on her.

She did not know what would happen when the morning came.

But she did know that her time to keep him safe was slipping through her fingers like river water, impossible to hold.

[CHAPTER 14] — THE FIRST KISS

Harrison sat by a small fire outside the lean-to, his shoulders hunched slightly against the cold, hands cupped together as he rubbed warmth into them. The fire crackled low, its glow barely enough to fend off the deepening chill of the coming winter. The camp beyond was quiet in the early morning, the sky still painted in the pale hues of dawn. The first true bite of the season had arrived, sharp and unrelenting, creeping into the bones of anyone unprepared for its arrival.

Tala approached, a heavy buffalo robe draped over one arm. She stopped just before him, the firelight flickering across her face. "You'll freeze before you're strong enough to walk proper," she said, her tone neutral as if the act meant nothing.

Harrison looked up at her, his blue eyes catching the light. He didn't reach for the blanket right away. Instead, he studied her, something unreadable in his gaze. Then, slowly, he took it, his fingers brushing against hers as he did.

The touch was brief, but it lingered in a way she had not expected. She forced herself not to pull away too quickly, not to acknowledge the warmth that passed between them despite the cold.

"Thank you," he murmured, his voice softer than usual, lacking the usual sarcasm or sharp wit.

[CHAPTER 14] — THE FIRST KISS

She gave a short nod and turned before he could say anything else, before she could find herself caught in something she had no name for.

The following morning, the sky was pale, streaked with the early hues of a sun reluctant to rise. The wind had calmed some, though the air still carried the bite of the changing season. Tala stood outside the lean-to, her arms folded against the cold as she watched Harrison pull himself up from where he had been resting. His movements were slow, careful, but he had gained more strength in the past few days. Enough, at least, to manage something more than lying around waiting for his body to mend.

"We're going out," she said.

He lifted an eyebrow at her, rubbing sleep from his face. "Out where?"

"Firewood." She didn't elaborate, didn't wait for his agreement. If he wanted to stay warm, he could help carry what would keep them that way.

He grumbled under his breath but didn't argue. She handed him a small hatchet before leading the way, her pace steady, though she kept it slow enough that he could keep up. They walked beyond the camp, past the last of the tipis, past the open stretch of land where the horses grazed, and into the thin grove of trees that stood at the base of the hills.

The world around them was quiet but alive in its own way—the rustling of dry leaves clinging to branches, the distant hoot of an owl still awake from the night, the faint stirrings of creatures burrowed beneath the frozen earth. The air smelled of pine and cold soil, of winter's breath waiting to settle over the land.

[CHAPTER 14] — THE FIRST KISS

Harrison worked beside her, gathering smaller branches first, his movements still careful, though his body no longer betrayed him the way it had in the days before. Tala watched him out of the corner of her eye, noting how he did not complain, how he did not fumble as much as she had expected.

"You learn quick," she remarked after a time.

He shot her a look, a smirk playing at his lips. "You sound surprised."

She shrugged, lifting a larger piece of wood and placing it in the growing pile. "Some men don't."

He chuckled, shaking his head. "You got a way of makin' a man feel real accomplished."

They worked in near silence for a while, the crisp air filling the space between them. Then, on a whim, Tala spoke a word in her own language, a simple one, something easy to pronounce. "Tubu," she said.

Harrison paused, glancing up at her. "What?"

"Tubu," she repeated. "It means 'wood.' Try it."

His brow furrowed, and he made an attempt, but the syllables tangled awkwardly in his mouth.

Tala smirked, shaking her head. "That was terrible."

"Well, hell, give me a chance," he said, adjusting his grip on the hatchet. "Say it again."

She did, and he tried once more, still butchering the pronunciation, though slightly less than before.

A sound rose in her chest before she could stop it—a laugh, sudden and unbidden. It had been weeks since she had

[CHAPTER 14] — THE FIRST KISS

laughed, truly laughed, and the surprise of it nearly startled her as much as it did him.

Harrison straightened slightly, a grin tugging at his lips. "That bad, huh?"

"Bad enough," she admitted, though the amusement still danced in her voice.

He watched her then, something shifting in his expression, something warmer than before. It was different from the way he usually looked at her—not the guarded wariness from when he had first woken, not the sharp, assessing gaze of a soldier studying his captors. This was something else. Something that made the space between them feel different, like a step had been taken toward something neither of them had intended.

She cleared her throat, turning back to the task at hand before the moment could settle too deeply. "Keep practicing," she said, her voice returning to its usual neutrality. "Maybe by the time the snow comes, you'll sound like less of a fool."

He chuckled, the warmth still lingering in his voice. "No promises."

The wind shifted through the trees, carrying the scent of winter and something else—something unspoken yet understood.

The wind swept through the trees, sending a flurry of golden leaves into the air. They spun and danced around them, caught in the autumn current, some settling at their feet while others clung to their clothes. Tala barely noticed as one landed in her hair, tangled among the loose strands

[CHAPTER 14] — THE FIRST KISS

that had come undone from her braid. She exhaled slowly, rolling a small branch between her fingers, letting the moment stretch in silence.

Harrison, crouched near their pile of gathered wood, saw it before she did. Without thinking, he reached out, his fingers brushing the stray leaf from her hair. It was a small thing, a fleeting movement, but then his hand lingered. His touch drifted, barely there, fingers tracing the side of her face as he tucked a loose strand of hair behind her ear.

His knuckles grazed her cheek, rough against the smoothness of her skin, and that was when she froze.

It wasn't fear that stilled her. It wasn't even caution. It was something deeper, something uncharted. A feeling she did not want to name.

The world around them seemed to slow, the rustling of the trees and the distant hum of the camp fading into something quieter. Her breath caught in her chest, her pulse a steady drum in her ears. Harrison didn't move away. His fingers remained at her temple, warm against the crisp autumn air, his touch neither hurried nor hesitant—simply there, waiting.

Tala became painfully aware of the space between them. Or rather, how little of it remained.

Harrison's blue eyes held hers, searching, uncertain yet intent. She knew he was giving her a choice, giving her time to pull away, to step back and let whatever this was drift into nothing. But she did not move.

She didn't know why she stayed.

[CHAPTER 14] — THE FIRST KISS

His breath was steady, though she could see the way his jaw tightened, the way his fingers curled slightly against her hair before he finally let his hand drop to his side. But instead of retreating, he leaned in, slow and deliberate, like he was stepping into unknown territory with the same measured caution he had used when learning to walk again.

Tala didn't think. She didn't weigh the consequences. She didn't remind herself of all the reasons she should stop this.

And then his lips met hers.

It was soft at first, hesitant, testing the ground beneath them. A whisper of warmth against the cold, his mouth barely brushing hers, as if waiting for permission. She didn't push him away.

The moment shifted. What had started as uncertain became something deeper, something neither of them were prepared for.

The kiss lingered, warm despite the biting chill in the air. Harrison's hand came to rest at her waist, light, not demanding, but there. The firewood at their feet, the changing season, the rest of the world—it all faded.

Until she suddenly pulled away.

Tala took a step back, her breath coming fast, uneven. Her heart pounded against her ribs, each beat a warning, each pulse reminding her of all the reasons this could not—must not—happen. She had let herself forget, just for a moment, what he was, what she was. But the truth hadn't changed. The world had not shifted to make this right.

[CHAPTER 14] — THE FIRST KISS

"This cannot be," she murmured, the words slipping out before she could stop them. It wasn't meant for him. It wasn't meant for anyone. It was a plea, a denial, a desperate attempt to rewrite what had just happened.

But even as she said it, she knew it was a lie.

Because it already was.

Harrison didn't move, didn't try to close the space she had created between them, but he also didn't look away. His breath was uneven, his lips parted, as if searching for words that would not come. The firewood lay forgotten at their feet, the crisp autumn air pressing in around them, but all Tala could focus on was the weight of what had just passed between them.

His blue eyes searched her face, and for the first time, she saw something other than defiance, other than stubbornness or frustration. There was uncertainty there, yes, but also something deeper, something that unsettled her more than anything else. He wasn't trying to convince her. He wasn't trying to make her stay. He was waiting.

Tala clenched her fists at her sides, grounding herself in the familiar sensation of her nails pressing into her palms. She needed to step away from this, from him, from the pull she had no business feeling.

"We should go back," she said finally, her voice steadier than she felt.

Harrison exhaled, the sound low, like he had been holding his breath. He nodded, slow, measured, as if he had expected nothing else. "Alright."

[CHAPTER 14] — THE FIRST KISS

She bent down and gathered the wood, hands moving faster than they needed to, as if the act of work could erase the last few minutes. Harrison crouched beside her, collecting his share without a word. The easy warmth that had existed between them earlier had vanished, replaced by something heavier, something neither of them seemed ready to name.

The walk back to camp was silent, the only sounds the rustling of the wind through the grass, the occasional crack of a twig beneath their steps. She did not look at him, and he did not try to speak. There was nothing to say that would change what had happened. And no words could undo what was already set in motion.

[CHAPTER 15] — THE WEIGHT OF DESIRE

Tala worked with single-minded focus, moving through the camp with a purpose that she told herself was entirely necessary. She knelt beside an older woman whose joints ached from the cold creeping into the land, grinding dried willow bark into a fine powder to steep in hot water. She checked the wounds of a young hunter who had taken a deep cut to his thigh while dressing a buffalo carcass. She mixed salves, checked stores of dried herbs, restocked bandages, and mended furs, anything that kept her hands moving, her mind occupied.

But no matter how much she busied herself, no matter how firmly she told herself that it had been a mistake, that moment by the fire refused to leave her.

Harrison's touch had been brief, just the brush of his fingers against her cheek, yet she could still feel it. The way he had hesitated, the way he had let her decide whether to pull away or not—those were not the actions of a man who took without thinking. She had expected something different from him, but she should not have. He was not like the soldiers she had seen before. And that unsettled her more than anything.

She did not go near the lean-to unless absolutely necessary. When she passed it, she kept her gaze forward, making sure her steps never slowed. When she did have to bring him food or check his wounds, she moved quickly,

[CHAPTER 15] — THE WEIGHT OF DESIRE

keeping her words few, avoiding his gaze. If he noticed, he did not push her.

But she knew he noticed.

Harrison's usual sharp remarks had grown quieter. He still spoke with the warriors who came to watch him, who tested him with their words, waiting for him to slip, but his answers were not as quick, not as biting. At night, when she worked by the fire preparing medicines, she could feel his gaze. It was never demanding, never insistent, but it was there.

And she hated that she wanted to look back.

Once, their eyes met across the firelight, and for a long moment, neither of them moved. The flames danced between them, casting flickering shapes across his face, softening the rough edges, making him look less like a soldier, less like a man who should not be here. Her breath caught, her pulse betraying her as she felt something pull tight in her chest.

Then, before she could let herself dwell on it, she looked away, turning back to the work in her hands.

It was foolish. It was dangerous.

It could not happen again.

The camp, already restless, grew more uneasy with each passing day. The warriors spoke of soldiers in the distance, of scouting parties seen along the river, of signs that their enemies were closing in. The men sharpened their weapons, the women prepared supplies for travel in case they needed to move quickly.

[CHAPTER 15] — THE WEIGHT OF DESIRE

Tala forced herself to focus on her duties. She pounded herbs into powder, stirred bitter teas, packed bandages in neat rolls. She spoke little, keeping her voice calm when others grew anxious, offering the medicine of words when the tinctures were not enough.

But no matter how hard she worked, no matter how much she tried to keep her mind steady, her thoughts betrayed her.

She told herself it had been a fleeting thing, a mistake born of the cold and the quiet, of the strange pull of the stars overhead.

But she knew better.

Because despite all her efforts, despite all her reasoning, the memory of that moment burned like an ember that refused to die.

One evening, Tala moved through the trees, her arms already filled with dry branches, the crisp bite of winter in the air as she searched for more. The earth beneath her feet was firm but not yet frozen, the golden remnants of autumn crunching softly with each step. The camp was only a short walk away, the distant hum of voices carrying on the wind, but here, among the trees, it was quiet. Peaceful.

Or at least, it had been.

The snap of a twig behind her sent a shiver down her spine, and before she could turn, a figure stepped into her path. Harrison.

He looked different now—stronger than before, his stance more sure, his frame no longer burdened by the weight of sickness. But it was not his physical state that gave

[CHAPTER 15] — THE WEIGHT OF DESIRE

him an edge of intensity. It was his eyes. Blue and stormy, filled with something she did not want to face.

Tala inhaled sharply and stepped to the side, as if to move past him, but he shifted, blocking her way. He was not aggressive, not forceful, but he stood firm, unmoving.

"You gonna pretend that didn't happen?" His voice was low, roughened by something deeper than frustration.

She swallowed, keeping her gaze on the ground, willing her hands not to tremble as she gripped the firewood tighter. "It was a mistake."

The words tasted bitter on her tongue, like an untruth spoken too many times. She forced herself to meet his gaze, but the fire there only burned hotter.

"A mistake?" His jaw tightened. "Is that what you're tellin' yourself?"

She nodded, willing herself to believe it. "There is no future for us," she said, softer than she intended. "It cannot be."

Harrison exhaled slowly, as if he had known she would say that but had hoped she wouldn't. His eyes searched hers, his shoulders rising and falling in steady breaths, like a man considering his next move in a losing fight.

Then, before she could step away, he reached out—slowly, carefully—his fingers wrapping around her wrist, not in restraint, but in something else. Something tender. He turned her hand over, palm to palm, then pressed it against his chest.

Tala's breath faltered.

[CHAPTER 15] — THE WEIGHT OF DESIRE

Beneath her fingers, his heart beat strong and steady, a rhythm that matched the warmth of his skin. It was not hurried, not frantic, but sure. Solid.

"Then why," he murmured, his voice quieter now, edged with something raw, "does it feel like the only thing in this world that feels right?"

She wanted to pull away. She needed to. But she didn't. Her fingers curled slightly, her pulse matching his, wild and uncertain.

His closeness was dangerous, not because of the way he looked at her, not even because of what the others would say if they saw—but because of how it made her feel. She had spent her whole life balancing between two worlds, never fully belonging to either. And now, here was a man who should have been nothing more than a captive, nothing more than an enemy—and yet, he saw her.

She had no answer to his question.

Because the truth was, she didn't want to let go.

Tala felt the weight of Harrison's gaze, the warmth of his chest beneath her hand, the unspoken words thick between them. The cold wind barely reached her, lost beneath the heat burning beneath her skin. Her pulse pounded in her ears, her breath shallow, caught somewhere between fear and something she did not dare name.

It was not just desire that held her there. It was something more. Something dangerous.

Then, without warning, the silence broke.

A gunshot split through the air like a jagged crack of lightning, sharp and final.

[CHAPTER 15] — THE WEIGHT OF DESIRE

Tala's breath sucked in, her body stiffening as the echo of the shot rolled across the plains. For a single heartbeat, the world held still—just long enough for her to see the change in Harrison's eyes, the moment his instincts sharpened, recognizing the sound for what it was.

Then the camp erupted into motion.

Shouting voices cut through the night, overlapping in urgency. Warriors surged past them, their feet pounding the hard-packed earth as they rushed toward the source of the sound. The campfires cast long, flickering shapes against the tipis, the once-peaceful hum of the night replaced by the clang of weapons being grabbed in haste.

Tala jerked her hand away from Harrison, the spell of the moment shattered.

She spun toward the camp, her breath tight in her chest. Men were calling to one another, some saddling horses in quick, practiced movements, others gripping bows and lances. Women pulled children close, guiding them toward safety, their faces drawn with worry but not panic. This was not the first time danger had come in the night.

Her mind snapped into focus, her breath steadying. She knew her place in this moment. She was not a warrior, but she was needed.

"We have to go," she said, turning toward the camp, her voice firm but steady.

Harrison caught her arm, his fingers pressing against her skin. "Tala—" His voice was laced with urgency, but he didn't pull her back, only searched her face.

[CHAPTER 15] — THE WEIGHT OF DESIRE

She met his gaze, saw the sharp awareness in his eyes. There was no time for hesitation. "Come with me," she said, softer this time, but no less resolute.

For a brief moment, he hesitated, not out of defiance, but calculation. He knew the risk of stepping into the heart of the camp now, surrounded by men who had already debated whether to let him live. But he also knew staying behind wasn't an option—not if the gunshot meant what they feared.

Without another word, he nodded.

Tala turned, leading him toward the camp at a fast but measured pace, her movements purposeful. Harrison kept close; his steps careful but determined despite his still-healing body. Around them, warriors rushed to their places, women gathered the children, elders issued quiet but firm commands. The air pulsed with the unspoken understanding that something was coming.

And as Tala guided Harrison deeper into the heart of the camp, she realized that whatever was about to happen, it would change everything.

[CHAPTER 16] — THE SOLDIERS DRAW NEAR

The camp was alive with movement, a frenzy of bodies weaving between the tipis and fires as warriors rushed toward the outskirts. The sharp gleam of weapons caught in the firelight—bows were strung, arrows notched, lances gripped tight. The air was thick with tension, voices low but urgent, every man scanning the dark horizon for any sign of their enemy.

Tala pulled Harrison to a halt near one of the outer tipis, her grip firm on his wrist. He stood stiff beside her, his breathing heavy but measured. No one had yet noticed him in the chaos, but that would not last long.

"They're watching the west and the north," Harrison murmured, his voice low, as his sharp eyes took in the warriors' positions. He was a soldier—injured or not, his instincts remained. "The shot came from the south."

Tala's lips pressed together. No one knew exactly where it had come from, and that was the problem. A single gunshot in the night could mean anything—a warning, an accident, a kill. But with the threat so near, there was no time to hesitate.

A sudden commotion drew their attention toward the edge of the camp, where a figure stumbled through the darkness. The warriors parted just enough to let him pass—a scout, his chest rising and falling in frantic, shallow breaths, his skin caked with sweat and dust.

[CHAPTER 16] — THE SOLDIERS DRAW NEAR

"They're coming," he gasped, gripping the arm of a nearby warrior for balance. "Soldiers. Just a couple of hours away from the river."

A ripple of sound passed through the camp, a murmur of voices blending into the crackling fires and the rustling of the night wind. The warriors turned as one, looking toward the council fire.

Tobáhā was already there, standing at the center of the gathering space, his broad frame unmoving as the others arrived. His gaze, dark and unreadable, moved from the scout to the warriors who followed, waiting for the full weight of the news to settle.

"I think they're searching for the white man." The scout spat into the dirt, wiping his mouth. "Not just a patrol. A full unit, moving steady."

Tala felt the breath leave her chest. They were looking for Harrison.

A hushed debate swelled like a tide around them. The council members arrived in hurried steps, elders pulling their furs tight against the cold. The warriors, tense with anticipation, formed a rough circle, their voices rising in fierce discussion. The campfires cast long flickering light on their faces, their expressions grim.

"We leave," a man near the back said, folding his arms across his chest. "There is no honor in staying and dying when we can move deeper into the land."

A few nodded in agreement. Others, less willing to abandon the homes they had built before the heart of winter set in, scowled.

[CHAPTER 16] — THE SOLDIERS DRAW NEAR

"We are not pack animals to scatter at the first scent of wolves," a warrior shot back. "We fight, or we die running."

Tobáhā listened, his face still unreadable.

"It is too late in the season to move now," one of the elders interjected, his voice weary but firm. "The herds have moved. The ground is too frozen to dig new caches. We would leave too much behind."

Nāhtöh stepped forward then, his anger barely contained. "Then we strike first."

Murmurs of agreement rumbled through the warriors nearest to him, their hands tightening on weapons. "Let them come looking," Nāhtöh continued, his voice sharp as flint. "We do not wait for the enemy to draw first blood."

Tobáhā remained silent, but the weight of the decision pressed into the space between them. Tala knew he was measuring every option, every risk.

And then another voice spoke, cutting through the tension like a blade.

"We use him."

All eyes turned to the man who had spoken, a warrior standing with arms crossed, his gaze pointed directly at Harrison.

"He is what they seek," the man continued. "Use him. Send him back to his people with a message—turn back, or face what waits for them here."

A few nodded, considering.

"They will not bargain for him," Nāhtöh snapped. "They will come for him. And they will come harder if they know he lives."

[CHAPTER 16] — THE SOLDIERS DRAW NEAR

Tobáhā finally moved, exhaling a long breath as he surveyed the men before him. "Then the question is this—do we flee? Do we fight? Or do we use the white man as a shield?"

Silence followed.

Tala's heart pounded in her chest as she turned her gaze toward Harrison. He stood at her side, his face unreadable, but his fists were clenched at his sides.

He knew that this was his fate being decided. And there was nothing he could do but listen to words he could not understand.

Tala turned her head slightly, meeting Harrison's gaze. He stood beside her, tense, his face unreadable, but she could see the way his jaw was clenched, the muscles in his arms tight beneath the worn fabric of his shirt. He had followed her here, had listened to the men argue over his life, and yet he had remained silent, waiting.

When she spoke, her voice was low, for him alone. "They believe your people are searching for you. Some want to fight before the soldiers arrive. Some say we should leave before they find us. Others—" She hesitated, the words catching. "Some want to use you. To send you back with a warning."

Harrison exhaled, a sound more of frustration than relief. His gaze flicked toward the warriors, the elders, the men who had just spoken of him as if he were nothing more than a tool to wield against the men he once called his own. His lips parted, and for a moment, she thought he might curse them, but instead, his voice came out firm, unwavering.

[CHAPTER 16] — THE SOLDIERS DRAW NEAR

"I have to go to them," he said.

Tala's stomach tightened. "No."

His eyes snapped to hers, frustration flashing across his face. "If I leave, they won't attack. But if they think I'm dead..." He trailed off, the implication settling between them like cold iron. "I won't be the reason they come in here, guns blazin'."

Tala felt something deep inside her twist at his words, something she did not want to name. If he left, he would be taken back into their ranks. Back to his regiment, back to the world that had brought him here in the first place. And if he left, she might never see him again.

She looked away, unable to hold his gaze. There was no argument she could give him that he would accept. What he said made sense, but sense had never mattered in war.

Before she could speak, before she could decide if she should even try to stop him, a warrior stepped forward from the gathered men. Tala caught the movement too late.

The blow came fast, a brutal strike to the side of Harrison's head. He crumpled instantly, his knees buckling beneath him, hands catching the dirt as he hit the ground. The campfire nearby flickered, sending its light glinting off the blade now hovering dangerously close to his throat.

"You don't get to decide your fate," the warrior spat, his voice a growl of fury.

Harrison's breath was labored as he struggled to push himself up, but the warrior pressed the tip of his blade against his skin, just below his jaw. A warning. One move and it would be the last he ever made.

[CHAPTER 16] — THE SOLDIERS DRAW NEAR

Tala reacted before she could think, before reason or fear could stop her. She stepped between them, her hand striking the warrior's wrist, pushing his blade away from Harrison's throat. The movement was swift, instinctive, but it sent a ripple through the gathered men.

The warrior's dark eyes snapped to hers, and for a long moment, neither of them spoke. The firelight painted his face in sharp lines of anger and disbelief.

"He is still a prisoner," the man growled. "Do not forget that."

Tala forced herself to meet his gaze, though her heart pounded like the war drums in the distance. "And we do not kill our prisoners."

Silence stretched between them, thick with the weight of unspoken words. The warrior did not lower his blade, but he did not move to strike again.

Harrison, still on the ground, shifted slightly, his fingers curling into the dirt. He did not speak, did not challenge the man who had knocked him down. He only looked up at Tala, his blue eyes sharp and unreadable.

She had made a choice tonight; one she could not take back. And for the first time, she was not sure if she had just saved him—or doomed them both.

Harrison let out a rough cough, trying to push himself up from the dirt, but his limbs betrayed him, weak from the strike. His breath was uneven, and the dull throbbing at his temple made it hard to focus. He barely registered the heat of the firelight on his skin or the murmuring voices of the warriors around him. What he did register was Tala.

[CHAPTER 16] — THE SOLDIERS DRAW NEAR

She was suddenly there beside him, her hands gripping his arms, steadying him before he could collapse again. Her touch was firm, grounding, the warmth of her fingers seeping through the worn fabric of his shirt. She didn't speak, didn't tell him to get up or to stay down. She simply held him there, her presence unwavering.

For a moment, everything else faded—the warriors, the fire, the tension hanging thick in the air. All that remained was the press of her fingers against his skin, the weight of her gaze on him. He forced himself to look up, blinking against the pain, and found her staring at him with something he couldn't quite place. It wasn't pity, nor was it mere concern. It was something deeper. Something raw.

He swallowed, his throat aching. "You didn't have to stand up for me," he rasped, his voice rough but steady.

Her fingers curled slightly, as if bracing against something unseen, before she exhaled, shaking her head. "I care for you. I wasn't about to stand by and watch."

The words weren't an admission, but they weren't a lie either. And that terrified him more than anything.

Harrison didn't know how long they stayed like that—seconds, minutes—but in that time, he saw something shift in her eyes. He saw the same thing he felt twisting inside his own chest. A pull. A question.

Would she fight for him? Against her own people, if it came to that?

The answer was dangerous. The answer could get them both killed.

[CHAPTER 16] — THE SOLDIERS DRAW NEAR

Before either of them could say another word, the distant sound of hooves carried across the cold night air. It was faint, but unmistakable. Then came the low murmuring of voices, urgent and clipped. A scout had returned.

Tala's grip on him vanished as she rose swiftly to her feet. The warrior who had struck Harrison turned sharply, eyes narrowing as another man strode into the firelight, his face streaked with dust from the trail.

"They are closer," the scout reported, breathless from his ride. "The whole regiment. Not far now—they are just arriving at the river. They look like they will probably camp there for a day or two before they cross."

The gathered warriors tensed, their murmurs shifting into something more urgent, more certain. Harrison saw it in their stances—the way their hands drifted toward their weapons, the way their bodies coiled as if preparing for war.

Tala took a half-step back, her hands clenched at her sides. She turned to look at Harrison, and in that moment, everything became clear.

This was no longer just a question of what to do with him. The soldiers were coming, whether for him or for something else. And the Comanche would not let them take anything without a fight.

[CHAPTER 17] — BETWEEN LOVE AND LOYALTY

The following morning, the air hung heavy with the unspoken weight of war. The camp stirred early, warriors sharpening their weapons, mothers pulling their children close, men and women reinforcing their lodges with what little they could spare. The scent of damp earth lingered in the air, carried by a wind that smelled of distant rain. It was the kind of morning that warned of change—not just in the weather, but in the course of fate itself.

Tala walked with purpose through the camp, her pace steady but her heart a storm inside her chest. She had not slept, not truly. Every time she closed her eyes, she saw blue ones staring back at her, searching for something she could not name. The night had stretched long, and when dawn broke, she knew where she had to go.

Tsénatokwa sat by the fire in front of her lodge, as she often did. The old healer's presence had always been a constant in Tala's life, a source of wisdom, a voice that never faltered. The flames before her crackled, licking at the damp wood, yet she remained still, unmoved by the world rushing around her. Others prepared for battle, but Tsénatokwa prepared for what came after.

Tala hesitated only a moment before stepping forward. She crouched beside the fire, pressing her hands against the earth as if to steady herself. The heat from the flames

[CHAPTER 17] — BETWEEN LOVE AND LOYALTY

warmed her skin, but it did nothing to quell the cold growing in her chest.

"I need advice," she said, her voice quieter than she intended.

Tsénatokwa did not look at her right away. The old woman reached for a small bundle of dried herbs beside her, slowly crumbling the leaves between her fingers before tossing them into the flames. The fire hissed in response, sending up a fragrant smoke that clung to the morning air.

Then, at last, Tsénatokwa turned her deep, knowing eyes to Tala.

"No," she said, shaking her head. "You do not need advice."

Tala's breath caught. The elder's words settled over her like a weight, heavy and certain.

"You already know your heart's answer," Tsénatokwa continued, her voice soft but unwavering.

Tala's fingers curled against her knees. The words struck deeper than she wanted them to. She had come for clarity, for wisdom, but all she had found was a truth she had been trying to deny.

"I don't—" Tala started, but the words felt hollow on her tongue. She swallowed, forcing herself to meet Tsénatokwa's gaze. "There is no choice here."

The healer hummed; her expression unreadable. "That is what you tell yourself."

Tala's throat tightened. "He is not—" she faltered, shaking her head. "He cannot stay."

"No," Tsénatokwa agreed, "he cannot."

[CHAPTER 17] — BETWEEN LOVE AND LOYALTY

Tala exhaled sharply, her frustration curling around her ribs. "Then why does it feel like I am the one being torn in two?" Her voice was quiet, but it carried the weight of something raw, something she did not dare name.

Tsénatokwa's gaze softened, just a little. "Because you are."

Silence stretched between them, broken only by the snap of the fire. Tala clenched her jaw, trying to push past the ache in her chest. She was Comanche. She had always known her place, her duty. But then why—why did it feel like everything was unraveling?

Tsénatokwa sighed, turning back to the fire. "Love between our kinds has never ended in anything but sorrow."

Tala flinched. The words struck like a blow, though she had expected them. They were not spoken in cruelty, but in truth. A truth as old as war itself.

Tsénatokwa stirred the fire with a stick, sending up a small plume of sparks that vanished into the air. Her face, lined with years of wisdom and grief, remained calm as she studied Tala. The younger woman sat stiffly across from her, hands pressed to her knees, waiting for the elder's words.

For a long time, there was only the crackle of the fire, the distant sounds of the camp stirring to life. Then, Tsénatokwa exhaled, shaking her head slightly.

"You think this has not happened before?" Her voice was quiet, but it carried weight. "You think you are the first to stand in this place, caught between two worlds?"

Tala swallowed. "No," she admitted. "But that does not mean—"

[CHAPTER 17] — BETWEEN LOVE AND LOYALTY

The elder held up a hand, silencing her. "Your mother thought as you do. She believed she could live in both places, walk in both skins. And she tried. But the world does not allow such things for long."

Tala's breath caught, her stomach twisting. Her mother's past was something she had always known, but Tsénatokwa had never spoken of it so plainly. "She never talked about it," Tala murmured. "Not really."

"She did not have to," the old woman said. "It was in her eyes. She carried her love for that man like a wound she could never let heal." She poked at the fire again, the flames licking hungrily at the dry wood. "For a time, perhaps, she thought she had found a way. But the river that separates our worlds is too deep, too swift. You can try to cross it, but sooner or later, it will pull you under."

Tala clenched her hands into fists. "Maybe she just wasn't strong enough," she said, though the words tasted bitter even as she spoke them.

Tsénatokwa's gaze sharpened. "Do not mistake love for weakness," she said firmly. "Your mother was strong. She fought for what she wanted, just as you do now. But the fight was never fair. It was never hers to win."

Tala looked away, her throat tight. "And you think I will lose, too."

"I think the world has already decided for you," the elder said softly. "And I think you already know it."

Silence stretched between them. The fire crackled, throwing flickering light against Tsénatokwa's face, making her look older, wearier.

[CHAPTER 17] — BETWEEN LOVE AND LOYALTY

Tala inhaled slowly. "Did she regret it?"

The elder watched her for a long moment. Then, with a sigh, she looked back into the fire.

"No," she said. "But it did not matter. Either way, your father disappeared."

Tala inhaled slowly, letting the words settle in her bones.

Tsénatokwa's gaze flickered toward her again. "You can still walk away."

Tala's chest ached, but she forced herself to nod. She knew what was expected of her. She knew what was right.

And yet, as she rose to her feet and stepped away from the fire, she felt no lighter. If anything, she felt the weight of her choices press even heavier against her.

She did not look back as she left.

But even as she walked away, she knew Tsénatokwa was still watching her.

And deep down, she knew the old healer was probably right.

The night stretched over the land like a vast, endless blanket, the only light coming from the pale sliver of moon and the faint glow of scattered campfires. Tala moved carefully, her steps light on the cold earth, her breath steady despite the storm raging inside her. She knew she was making a mistake—she had told herself so a dozen times since leaving Tsénatokwa's fire. But knowing did not stop her feet from moving toward Harrison's lean-to. It did not stop her from wanting—against all reason—to see him one last time before everything changed.

[CHAPTER 17] — BETWEEN LOVE AND LOYALTY

She pulled back the flap of his shelter with slow deliberation, stepping inside as quietly as possible. But he was awake. He was waiting.

Harrison sat up, his blue eyes catching the dim light, watching her with an expression she couldn't quite name. Relief? Worry? Something deeper, something that made her breath come faster. He didn't speak right away, just studied her, his features unreadable. The air between them felt impossibly small, charged with everything unsaid, with the knowledge that the world outside this lean-to would never allow what lingered between them.

"Why did you come?" His voice was rough, quiet, edged with something that sent a shiver down her spine.

Tala opened her mouth, but nothing came at first. She had thought she knew, had convinced herself she had a reason. But now, standing in front of him, she realized she had none—not one that made sense. Not one she was ready to admit.

"I don't know," she finally said, and the truth of it burned.

Harrison exhaled sharply, shaking his head as if she'd just made things harder for him, though his body leaned ever so slightly toward hers. His fingers lifted, hesitated in the space between them before brushing against hers. A touch so light it could have been a mistake. But it wasn't.

"If I had met you in another life," he murmured, his voice low, raw with something unspoken, "I would have fought kingdoms for you."

The words struck her deeper than she wanted to admit, a tremor running through her. She had spent her life knowing what lines could never be crossed, what things were never meant to be. But standing here, with him, in this stolen moment where the rest of the world did not exist, none of that mattered.

"And in this life?" she asked, her voice barely above a whisper.

Harrison looked at her for a long moment, his eyes dark, conflicted, something desperate flickering in them. His fingers curled around hers, just enough to keep her there. His breath was unsteady when he answered, his voice nothing more than a hushed confession.

"In this life, I'd still fight. Even if I knew I'd lose."

Harrison didn't hesitate this time. He closed the space between them, his hands catching her waist, pulling her against him with a force that left no room for doubt. His lips found hers, not soft, not questioning, but desperate, aching, as if he was trying to capture something fleeting, something already slipping through his fingers.

Tala gasped against his mouth, but she didn't pull away. Her body betrayed her, pressing closer, her fingers tangling into his hair as if she could hold onto this moment, make it real, make it last. His grip tightened, strong and unyielding, his warmth sinking into her, filling the cold, empty spaces she had never realized were there.

The world outside didn't exist. Not the war, not the lines drawn in blood, not the certainty that this could never be. There was only the heat between them, the fire that burned away everything else. She could feel his heartbeat,

[CHAPTER 17] — BETWEEN LOVE AND LOYALTY

rapid and unsteady, matching her own. His breath came hot against her lips as they broke apart for just a second before he kissed her again, deeper this time, as if afraid she would disappear if he let her go.

For one fleeting second, they allowed themselves to forget.

Forget the warriors sharpening their weapons. Forget the soldiers waiting at the river. Forget the future, the past, the impossible gulf between them.

But then the drums started.

A low, pulsing rhythm that carried through the night like a heartbeat, steady and unrelenting.

Tala ripped herself away from him, breathless, her pulse hammering wildly—not from the kiss, but from the crushing weight of reality slamming back into her chest.

Harrison stood still, his hands clenched at his sides, his breath uneven, but he understood. The moment was over. The world had returned.

Outside, voices rose in tense conversation, warriors preparing for what they all knew was coming.

By dawn, everything would change.

[CHAPTER 18] — THE REGIMENT ARRIVES

Tobáhá's gaze was unreadable as he studied Harrison, then turned to Tala. He exhaled slowly before lifting his hand—a silent command for the voices to quiet.

"We will let him go," Tobáhá said at last. His voice carried, strong and sure, leaving no room for argument. "But hear me, soldier—if you ride to them and turn against us, your life is forfeit." His gaze darkened. "And so is hers."

Tala's breath caught, but she did not move.

Harrison's jaw tightened. He gave a slow nod. "I understand."

The chief's gaze lingered on them both before he turned to the warriors. "Prepare a horse for him. And watch the hills." His voice dropped, firm with warning. "If this is a trick, we will not be taken unaware."

Tobáhá paused then, his gaze settling once more on Tala. The weight of his decision was evident in the slow breath he took before speaking again. "You will go with him."

A ripple of murmurs spread through the gathered warriors. Tala stiffened.

"If he speaks for peace, let them see that he is not alone," Tobáhá continued. "If he turns against us, you will be the first to pay the price." His dark eyes bore into hers. "If he betrays us, kill him."

[CHAPTER 18] — THE REGIMENT ARRIVES

Tala swallowed hard, her mind racing. Sending her with Harrison was both a test and a threat—Tobáhā was not granting trust, he was ensuring that no matter the outcome, the Comanche would not be at a disadvantage. She was to be both a witness and an executioner, should it come to that.

Harrison's head turned sharply toward her, his brows furrowing. "That ain't necessary," he said, his voice tense. "I ain't leading you into a trap."

"It is necessary," Tobáhā said simply. "A man will say anything to save his own life. But actions speak louder than words." His gaze flicked to Tala once more. "She will know the truth of this before we do."

Tala inhaled deeply, forcing her expression to remain neutral. There was no use in arguing. The chief's word was final.

A warrior stepped forward, leading two horses by the reins. Tala recognized the one they handed to her—it was a sturdy, swift mare, trained for endurance, not just speed. Harrison's horse was lean but strong, a creature that had been captured from the whites long ago.

She turned toward Harrison. His jaw was set, tension lining his features, but he didn't fight the decision. He only looked at her, a question in his gaze.

"Let's go," she said, swinging onto her horse.

Harrison followed suit, adjusting in the saddle with ease, though she could see the stiffness in his movements. He was not yet fully healed, and this ride would push him to his limits.

[CHAPTER 18] — THE REGIMENT ARRIVES

Tobáhā stepped forward once more, his expression like carved stone. "If you do not return by sundown, we will assume the worst."

Tala nodded. There was no need to ask what that meant. If they did not return, war would follow.

Without another word, she nudged her horse forward. Harrison fell into step beside her. As they rode from the camp, the eyes of the people bore into their backs, watching, waiting.

She did not look back.

The horses snorted uneasily as Tala and Harrison rode past the last ridge that separated the Comanche camp from open land. The morning sun glowed faintly behind wisps of gray clouds, casting a dull light over the prairie. A biting wind carried the scent of distant water and earth, but it was the weight of silence that pressed hardest on them both.

Then, just beyond a low rise, the cavalry appeared.

Rows of blue-coated soldiers stretched across the open plain, moving at a steady pace toward the camp. The metallic glint of rifles and sabers caught the weak sunlight, and the sound of hooves striking frozen earth sent a low tremor through the ground. The regiment was disciplined, their formation tight, and their purpose clear. They had come for war.

Tala's stomach tightened, her grip on the reins firming. She stole a glance at Harrison, whose jaw had set into a hard line. There was no hesitation in his movements as he nudged his horse forward, lifting both hands high in surrender.

[CHAPTER 18] — THE REGIMENT ARRIVES

"Hold your fire!" he called, his voice carrying over the wind. "It's me! Sergeant Grant!"

The cavalry wavered. A ripple of uncertainty passed through the ranks, the front line slowing, their rifles still raised but unfired. Some of the men exchanged wary glances, their grips tightening on their weapons. They did not lower them.

From the center of the line, a voice rang out, sharp and commanding. "Sergeant Grant?"

Harrison exhaled, a flicker of relief in his eyes. " Sergeant Mercer!" he called back, his voice strong, urgent. "Stand down! I am not their prisoner—I came to talk!"

A murmur ran through the soldiers. Tala could see it now—the uncertainty in their faces, the doubt. They did not know if he was returning as a soldier or as a traitor.

Mercer's horse stepped forward, the sergeant's coat whipping in the wind. His gaze locked onto Harrison, then flicked to Tala beside him. His mouth twisted slightly, but his expression remained unreadable. "Explain yourself," he demanded.

But before Harrison could speak, another voice rang out.

"OPEN FIRE!"

The words were sharp as a knife, followed by the deafening crack of gunfire. The command had not come from Mercer—but it didn't matter. The order had been given.

Tala's breath caught as the first shots rang out, the air around them splitting apart with a deafening roar. The first

[CHAPTER 18] — THE REGIMENT ARRIVES

bullets struck the ground near their horses, sending up plumes of dust and dirt. A sharp whizz cut past her ear, close enough that she felt the wind of it.

Harrison shouted; his voice lost in the chaos. "NO! HOLD YOUR FIRE!" He waved his arms wildly, his horse rearing back as he fought for control. "STOP, DAMN YOU! IT'S ME!"

But the regiment had already committed to battle. More shots followed in rapid succession, the air thick with smoke and the acrid scent of gunpowder.

Tala didn't hesitate. She grabbed Harrison's arm, yanking him hard. "Move!" she snapped, spurring her horse toward a small cluster of boulders for cover.

The ground exploded beside them as bullets struck dirt and stone, one shot grazing the flank of Harrison's horse. The animal shrieked and stumbled, nearly throwing him, but he gritted his teeth and stayed mounted, his face dark with fury and disbelief.

They reached cover in a breathless rush, skidding to a halt behind the rocks. Harrison turned, his breath coming fast and hard, his hands shaking. His voice was raw. "They didn't even hesitate." His eyes darted back to the soldiers, to the men he had once called brothers. "I tried—I tried to stop them."

Tala watched him, chest heaving. She had seen many betrayals in her life. She had never seen one wound a man like this.

"Now you know," she murmured, her voice low, almost bitter. "You are not one of them anymore."

[CHAPTER 18] — THE REGIMENT ARRIVES

Harrison's gaze met hers. Something deep inside him splintered, and for the first time, she saw it—he wasn't just a soldier anymore. He was something else. Something lost.

[CHAPTER 19] — A CHOICE OF THE HEART

The acrid scent of burning powder clung to the cold morning air, settling into the earth like a warning. Smoke curled from the rifle barrels of the blue-coated soldiers, drifting in thin wisps toward the sky. Horses pawed at the ground, their nostrils flaring at the lingering tension, their riders shifting uneasily in their saddles. The gunfire had stopped, but silence carried its own kind of violence.

Tala stood frozen behind the jagged rock that had shielded them from the bullets, her heart pounding in her chest. In one direction lay the Comanche camp—the only home she had ever known. With her stood the man she had come to love, who now faced his own people, possibly as a traitor. The weight of that truth pressed down on her like a stone.

Harrison positioned himself between her and the regiment, his breath coming hard and fast. His hand hovered near his holster, not to draw, but to steady himself. He lifted his voice, strong despite the rawness in his throat. "Hold your fire!" The wind carried his words across the open plain, but no one moved. The cavalry's hesitation was palpable, the brief fury of battle giving way to confusion. They had been prepared for war, not for the sight of one of their own standing beside the enemy.

He turned toward his commander, searching for the man who still had the power to stop this before it spiraled

[CHAPTER 19] — A CHOICE OF THE HEART

further. "Sergeant Mercer! Captain Lockwood! Stand your men down!" His voice cracked with urgency. "There doesn't have to be a fight!"

For a long moment, no one answered.

Then, from the front of the formation, a rider pushed his horse forward. The man's uniform was crisp despite the dust, his officer's insignia gleaming against the dull morning light. His face was lined, unreadable, his mouth set in a firm line as he reined his mount to a halt. The soldiers around him stiffened at his presence.

Captain Lockwood.

He surveyed the scene with a calculating eye, his gaze settling on Harrison. For a long moment, he said nothing. The wind stirred between them, ruffling the flags attached to the regiment's lances. When he finally spoke, his voice was flat, almost tired, as if the decision had already been made.

"You're coming back with us."

The words hit harder than any gunfire. Harrison felt them settle in his chest, sharp as a blade. His mouth felt dry, his mind racing through the possibilities. There was no room for argument in Lockwood's tone, no hint of hesitation. It was an order.

Tala shifted behind him, and without thinking, Harrison stepped slightly closer to her, shielding her from their view. His body had been trained to obey a command like that, but everything inside him rebelled at it now. His place was no longer there.

[CHAPTER 19] — A CHOICE OF THE HEART

Lockwood's gaze flicked to the woman at his side. "And what of her?" His tone was neutral, but there was something weighted beneath it.

Harrison's throat tightened. He turned his head just slightly, just enough to see Tala out of the corner of his eye. She was watching him, her face unreadable, but he could feel the tension in her body, the silent storm raging within her.

He had known this moment would come. He had known, and yet, it still felt like a loss.

Tala's heartbeat pounded in her ears, the weight of the moment pressing down on her like the heavy skies before a storm. She could feel the unspoken expectation in the air, the invisible tether that bound her to her people, pulling her back toward them. If she turned now, if she walked away from Harrison and returned to the camp, no one would question her place. No one would doubt where her loyalty lay.

But she already knew.

The choice had been made long before this moment, long before gunfire shattered the morning air. Perhaps it had been decided the moment she knelt beside him, pressing a damp cloth to his fevered brow. Or the first time she saw him struggle to walk, refusing to accept his weakness. Or maybe it was in the way he had looked at her that night, on the ridge beneath the stars, when neither of them had spoken, but everything had been understood.

She stepped forward.

"I will go with you," she said, her voice steady.

[CHAPTER 19] — A CHOICE OF THE HEART

Murmurs rippled through the ranks of soldiers before them, low and uncertain, but the only response that mattered came from Harrison. He turned sharply, his blue eyes locking onto hers, searching. She saw the conflict there, the warring emotions, the fear and the quiet relief. His hands curled into fists at his sides.

"Tala..." His voice was rough, but he didn't finish.

She lifted her chin, unwavering. "I will go."

A muscle tightened in his jaw, and then he exhaled, his shoulders straightening as if accepting the weight of what she had just done. He turned back to Lockwood, whose face remained unreadable. The Captain studied them both, his expression sharp with calculation.

"I need to tell her people," Harrison said. "I need to go with her."

Lockwood's brows lifted, his fingers tightening briefly on the reins of his horse. He glanced back at the men behind him, some still gripping their rifles, their faces taut with suspicion. Then he returned his gaze to Harrison.

"You're asking a lot," he said, his voice low. "I don't know if you realize that."

Harrison's mouth pressed into a firm line. "I do."

Lockwood inhaled slowly, then exhaled through his nose. He turned his gaze to Tala, measuring her, before nodding once. "Then I'm coming too."

Harrison stiffened slightly. "That might not—"

Lockwood cut him off. "I will not march my men into war blind. If we're going to have a parley, I'll be part of it. And I'll bring a small patrol. Six men. No more."

[CHAPTER 19] — A CHOICE OF THE HEART

Tala forced herself to remain still, her pulse thrumming. She knew how her people would react to this. Warriors already burned for battle. The presence of any soldiers, no matter how few, would stoke the flames. But she also knew that if Harrison returned alone, without the weight of authority behind him, they might not listen at all.

Harrison exhaled, then gave a slow nod. "Alright."

Lockwood turned slightly in his saddle. "Sergeant Mercer," he called.

A tall, square-shouldered man trotted forward, his eyes darting warily to Tala before settling on Lockwood.

"Sir?"

Lockwood's gaze was firm. "No attacks on the Comanche while we're gone. We return by tomorrow afternoon. No later. Otherwise attack."

Mercer's brow furrowed. He opened his mouth as if to protest, but one sharp look from Lockwood silenced him.

"Yes, sir," Mercer said, though his voice carried a hint of reluctance.

Lockwood turned his horse back toward Harrison and Tala, expression unreadable. "Then let's ride."

As they rode back into the village, the weight of what she had done settled heavily on Tala's chest. The horses moved at a slow, deliberate pace, the small patrol of soldiers behind them keeping their hands close to their weapons but following her lead. Harrison rode beside her, his expression unreadable, but she could feel the tension in his body, the way he braced for what was coming.

[CHAPTER 19] — A CHOICE OF THE HEART

The village had seen them before they even crossed into its heart. Warriors stood at the ready, their grips tight on their spears and bows, their gazes sharp with suspicion. The presence of the white men among them sent a ripple of unease through the camp. Women pulled their children back, elders straightened, their faces carved from stone.

When they came to a stop, the silence was thick, charged. Then, a murmur swept through the gathered crowd like a rising wind.

Tobáhā stepped forward, his gaze unreadable as he took in the sight before him. But it was Nāhtöh who spoke first.

"You would bring them here?" Nāhtöh's voice was sharp, a blade honed by fury. He stepped forward, his gaze burning into Tala, disbelief twisting his features. "You would ride with them? Bring them into our home?"

Before Tala could speak, his voice dropped lower, thick with something harsher than anger. "You would betray your own blood?"

Gasps rippled through the gathered crowd, warriors shifting on their feet, their expressions flickering between anger and sorrow. Tala did not flinch, though his words cut deep, deeper than she cared to admit.

"I have betrayed no one. I had to bring them," she said, her voice steady.

"You had to?" Nāhtöh scoffed, his hands curling into fists at his sides. "For him?" He cast a scornful glance at Harrison, then spit onto the ground. "You did this for a soldier of the white men?"

"I did what I must," she said, her chin lifting.

[CHAPTER 19] — A CHOICE OF THE HEART

"What you must?" Nāhtöh barked a laugh, shaking his head. "Then you have chosen, Tala. And it is not us."

She swallowed hard, her throat tightening. She had known this moment would come, had known the cost, but standing here, before her people, the finality of it twisted in her chest.

Tobáhā's gaze rested on her for a long moment, his expression unreadable. "And what is it you are saying, Tala?" His voice was quieter than Nāhtöh's, but it carried a weight that pressed down on her like stone.

Tala exhaled slowly. "I will go with them."

There. The words were out. Spoken aloud, undeniable.

Another ripple moved through the gathered warriors, and she could see the way some faces darkened, how others turned away. A few of the elders exchanged knowing glances, as if they had seen this path before, as if they had known it would end here.

Tsénatokwa, the elder healer, stepped forward. Her lined face was solemn, her eyes filled with something quieter, deeper—sorrow. "You know what this means, child," she said softly.

Tala felt the weight of the words before she even nodded.

"I know."

Tsénatokwa's gaze did not waver. "Once you go, you will not return."

A hush fell over the camp, heavier than before, and for the first time, true finality settled in Tala's bones. This was

[CHAPTER 19] — A CHOICE OF THE HEART

not a choice she could unmake. She had already crossed the threshold, and there was no path back.

Harrison's fingers brushed against hers, tentative at first, as if afraid she might still change her mind. His touch was warm despite the chill in the air, steady even as uncertainty swirled between them. Tala did not pull away, but she did not grasp his hand either. Not yet. Her heart pounded with a heaviness she had never known, the weight of her choice pressing into her ribs like a vice.

Captain Lockwood sat stiffly in the saddle, his gaze unreadable, but the tension in his jaw betrayed his thoughts. He did not approve—his silence made that clear. But he said nothing, merely observing as if waiting for her to falter, to second-guess herself, to turn back. When she did not, his fingers twitched on the reins, a brief movement, but one Tala did not miss. He was a man who had spent a lifetime issuing orders, and here she was, defying the expectations of both his world and her own.

A low murmur rose among the warriors, their voices thick with grief, with disbelief, with the finality of what was happening. Tala had known they would not understand, but hearing their sorrow woven into the wind made her breath catch in her throat. She dared to glance around her, taking in the faces of the people she had called family—faces that now looked at her as though she had already become something else. Nāhtöh's expression was dark, unreadable save for the anger she knew simmered beneath the surface. Others turned away, unwilling or unable to watch her leave.

And Tsénatokwa—her gaze held no anger, only sorrow. The old woman stood apart from the others, hands

[CHAPTER 19] — A CHOICE OF THE HEART

clasped in front of her, the lines on her face deeper in the flickering torchlight. She had seen this before. Tala could read it in her eyes. A story playing out again, an ending already written.

Tala swallowed hard, forcing herself to turn her gaze away, to take in the land one final time. The campfires flickered like stars against the earth, the tipis standing strong against the wind, the horses moving restlessly in the darkness. She had walked these paths since she was a child. She had learned to track and hunt here, had learned the songs of her people, had listened to the stories passed down for generations. And now, she would leave it behind.

Her hands curled into fists at her sides. A part of her ached to stay, to reach out and hold onto the life she had always known. But another part of her—something deeper, something undeniable—pulled her forward. It had begun the moment she chose to heal him. It had only grown stronger with each passing day.

She turned to Harrison. His blue eyes, so different from any she had known before, held no doubt. He was not asking her to leave. He had not spoken a word to convince her. But the moment she looked at him, she knew with certainty—wherever he went, she would follow.

The choice was made.

And there was no turning back.

[CHAPTER 20] — THE COMANCHE BRIDE

As the camp gathered near the council fire, the air was thick with unease. The warriors stood tense, some gripping their spears, others watching with arms folded, their expressions unreadable. Tobáhā sat cross-legged before the fire, his face carved with deep lines of thought, his dark eyes fixed on the man who now stood before him. Captain Lockwood remained mounted for a moment, his posture rigid, his mouth set in a firm line, before finally dismounting, his boots hitting the frozen earth with purpose.

Tala stood between them, feeling the weight of both worlds pressing down on her shoulders. The silence stretched unbearably before she turned to face the chief.

"The white soldiers wish to speak of peace," she said in Comanche, her voice even, though her heart pounded. "They do not want war—not now."

Tobáhā studied Lockwood for a long moment before lifting his chin slightly. "Peace," he repeated, the word tasting foreign in his mouth. He let it settle between them before glancing at Tala. "Tell him I will listen. But no white man has ever come offering peace without wanting something in return."

Tala swallowed, then turned to Lockwood. "He says he will listen, but he does not trust your words."

Lockwood exhaled sharply through his nose. "I wouldn't expect him to." He straightened slightly, his eyes

[CHAPTER 20] — THE COMANCHE BRIDE

never leaving Tobáhā's. "Tell him that my men came looking for Sergeant Grant, not for war. Our orders were to retrieve him, not to attack. I ordered my men to fire, and for that, I take full responsibility. I made the decision, and it was the wrong one."

Tala translated, watching the way Tobáhā's expression remained impassive. The older man did not react at first, then finally leaned forward, resting his elbows on his knees.

"Their guns are always quick," Tobáhā muttered. "They never stop to ask before they take."

"They did not kill," Tala offered softly.

Tobáhā snorted, his dark eyes flicking toward her before returning to Lockwood. "Not for lack of trying."

Lockwood let out a slow breath. "I cannot change the past, but I can ensure that no more blood is spilled—at least for now. Winter is almost here. We have no desire to fight through the cold. We will move our regiment back to our fort, away from your people, if you agree to leave us be."

Tobáhā's gaze sharpened. "And what will happen when spring comes?"

Tala translated, her voice quiet, but inside, her heart thundered. She knew what her people feared. They had seen it before—treaties spoken, handshakes given, only for white soldiers to return with more men, more weapons, more destruction.

Lockwood hesitated for the first time, his fingers flexing at his sides. "Spring is not a promise I can make. But I can offer a truce for the winter. My men will not come here. We will not hunt here. We will not seek to take land."

[CHAPTER 20] — THE COMANCHE BRIDE

Tobáhā narrowed his eyes. "And in return?"

Lockwood's gaze flickered toward Harrison, then back to Tala. "In return, we take Sergeant Grant and his woman with us."

Tala felt the words settle in her chest like a stone, heavy and final. She knew it was coming, but hearing it spoken aloud made it real.

Tobáhā exhaled through his nose, looking at her now. His gaze did not hold the anger of the others, nor the sorrow of Tsénatokwa. It was something else—resignation, perhaps, or understanding.

"The choice has already been made," he said quietly. "She is no longer one of us."

Tala swallowed, lowering her gaze.

Tobáhā turned back to Lockwood. "You will leave our lands within two days. And if one of your soldiers returns before spring—" his voice darkened, low and certain, "—we will show no mercy."

Tala translated, her voice steady, and Lockwood nodded. "Understood."

For a moment, neither man spoke. The fire crackled between them, sending sparks into the dark sky. Then, finally, Tobáhā lifted his chin.

"The white soldiers will go. My people will not follow." His gaze flickered to Tala once more. "And she will walk the path she has chosen."

Tala felt the finality of it in her bones.

Lockwood gave a curt nod. "Then we have an agreement."

[CHAPTER 20] — THE COMANCHE BRIDE

The warriors around them did not cheer, did not celebrate. This was not a victory. It was merely survival.

Tala stood silent, feeling the cold settle deep in her chest. There was no going back now.

Tobáhā's gaze was unreadable as he gestured for Tala to follow him away from the gathering. The village was still stirring with unease, warriors casting dark glances toward the soldiers who remained mounted nearby. Even with the truce negotiated, tension clung to the air like an impending storm. Tala hesitated before stepping after the chief, feeling the weight of what she was about to leave behind pressing against her ribs.

They walked a short distance, just far enough that their voices would not be easily heard by the others. Tobáhā turned to face her, his lined face solemn. He did not speak at first, only studying her as if memorizing the sight of her. Then, at last, he broke the silence.

"If you are to go," he said, his voice heavy with something deeper than authority, "you must not leave as a prisoner. Nor as a woman with no standing."

Tala frowned slightly, her pulse steady but unsure. "I do not leave as a prisoner," she said carefully. "It is my choice."

Tobáhā nodded once. "Then leave with honor," he said, his tone firm, absolute. "I will not have the soldiers think they can take you as if you are something to be claimed. If you leave, you leave as a wife."

[CHAPTER 20] — THE COMANCHE BRIDE

Tala's breath caught. For a moment, she thought she had misunderstood. But the look in Tobáhā's eyes told her she had not.

"You wish to marry us?" she asked, her voice quieter than she intended.

His gaze did not waver. "It is the only way," he said simply. "You would be seen as a Comanche woman, not a stray caught between worlds. You will be bound to your choice, and so will he."

Tala swallowed hard. She had known there was no going back, but now, hearing the words aloud, the finality of it struck deeper than she expected.

Tobáhā's voice softened just slightly. "Your mother would have wished it," he said. "She chose her own path, as you now choose yours. But she would not want you to leave without standing."

Tala's throat tightened. She nodded once, but her mind was already racing.

She turned back toward the waiting figures, her steps measured as she walked toward Harrison. He was speaking with Captain Lockwood, his stance tense, though his gaze softened slightly when he saw her approach. He seemed relieved to see her, but that relief turned to curiosity when he saw the expression on her face.

"What is it?" he asked, voice low.

She wet her lips, glancing briefly toward Tobáhā before meeting Harrison's eyes. "Tobáhā says that if I am to go, I must not go as a prisoner or as a woman without standing."

[CHAPTER 20] — THE COMANCHE BRIDE

She took a steadying breath. "He wishes to marry us before we leave."

Harrison blinked, clearly caught off guard. He exhaled sharply, rubbing a hand over his jaw, as if searching for the right words. "That's..." He let out a dry laugh, shaking his head. "Damn, that's not what I expected."

Tala's stomach twisted slightly. "If you do not wish it—"

"No," he cut in, his voice firm but not unkind. His blue eyes met hers, something unshaken settling into his expression. "I just..." He ran a hand through his hair before exhaling again, slower this time. "Are you sure?"

She hesitated. Was she sure? The moment felt too big, too heavy to grasp all at once. But deep in her chest, beneath all the fear and uncertainty, she already knew the answer.

"Yes."

Harrison studied her for a long moment before nodding. His hand reached for hers, fingers brushing lightly against hers before tightening. "Then so am I."

Behind them, a sharp sound of boots striking the earth drew their attention. Captain Lockwood had stepped closer, his face drawn into a look of grim disbelief.

"This is madness," Lockwood muttered, shaking his head. "Harrison, do you understand what this means? What it will mean when we return?"

Harrison turned to face him, his grip on Tala's hand tightening slightly. "I do," he said without hesitation.

Lockwood exhaled through his nose; his jaw clenched. He looked between them, then at Tobáhā, before finally pressing his lips into a hard line. "I'll stay," he said, though his tone made it clear he was not pleased. "I'll observe. But don't expect me to celebrate this."

Tala lifted her chin. "Thank you for staying. Know that I do not expect anything from you."

Lockwood gave her a long look but said nothing more.

Tobáhā turned to the gathered warriors and elders. "It will be done before the sun rises."

Murmurs rippled through the camp, a mix of shock, disapproval, and acceptance. The weight of the moment settled deep in Tala's chest, pressing against her ribs like something too vast to contain. She felt the warmth of Harrison's fingers wrapped around hers, steady and unyielding.

By dawn, she would no longer be Tala of the Comanche. She would be Tala, the wife of a soldier.

The camp gathered in solemn silence, warriors and elders standing in a loose circle around the ceremonial fire, their faces carved from stone. No one spoke, no one moved unnecessarily. The only sound was the wind moving through the trees and the distant murmur of horses in their enclosures. This was no time for celebration, only transition.

Tala stood beside Harrison, her breath shallow, aware of every watchful gaze upon her. This was not just the binding of two souls—it was the closing of one life and the uncertain beginning of another. She lifted her chin, forcing herself to stand tall as Tobáhā stepped forward, his expression unreadable in the flickering firelight.

[CHAPTER 20] — THE COMANCHE BRIDE

A woman approached from behind, draping a ceremonial blanket over Tala's shoulders, its heavy weave warm and grounding. The fabric, rich with reds and deep earth tones, was the mantle of a wife, the final mark of her belonging. Except she did not belong, not anymore. The weight of it settled on her like an unspoken truth—this would be the last gift from her people.

A warrior stepped forward, placing a long knife at Harrison's feet. The blade gleamed in the firelight, its edge sharp, its purpose clear. It was not meant for battle, not this night. It was a test.

Harrison's jaw tightened, having been told by Tala what was expected of him. Slowly, he knelt, pressing his palm flat against the blade, the metal cold beneath his skin. It was a vow, one that could not be spoken but must be felt— to protect the woman beside him with everything he had, or to die trying.

Tobáhā watched, waiting, and when Harrison did not waver, he gave a small nod of approval. The knife was lifted away, the moment sealed.

Then, the chief stepped forward once more, holding out two objects. The first was a small carved figure, its form etched from wood, smoothed by time and careful hands. It was a representation of the land; of the life Harrison would never fully understand but would now be tied to through Tala. The second was a woven sash, red and blue, the colors of both blood and sky—strength and eternity.

"These are gifts of honor," Tobáhā said, his voice steady, but heavy with something else—finality. "One for the past. One for the path ahead."

[CHAPTER 20] — THE COMANCHE BRIDE

Tala reached out first, her fingers brushing against Harrison's as she passed him the woven sash. His grip lingered, as if anchoring himself in the only thing that made sense in this moment. Then, he placed the wooden figure into her hands, his gaze searching hers, unspoken words thick in the space between them.

A murmur of agreement came from the gathered elders, and Tsénatokwa stepped forward, raising her hands to the sky before lowering them to the earth. Her voice was soft but carried through the night, a blessing that had been spoken over generations of Comanche unions.

"The earth beneath your feet bears witness," she murmured, her gaze sweeping over them. "The sky above sees your promise. The wind will carry your names, and the rivers will remember this night. You are bound, now and always."

A length of leather cord was brought forth, looped around Tala and Harrison's wrists. Tobáhā took the ends and pulled them tight, tying the knot with deliberate care. There was no breaking this vow, not without severing something deeper than words.

The silence stretched, heavy and absolute. No applause, no cheers. This was not a time for joy, not when Tala was stepping away from the people who had raised her, the land that had cradled her. It was a blessing, yes—but also a farewell.

The fire crackled, sending embers drifting into the cold pre-dawn air.

Tala inhaled slowly, feeling the leather tight around her wrist, feeling the warmth of Harrison's pulse against hers.

[CHAPTER 20] — THE COMANCHE BRIDE

She was no longer just Tala of the Comanche. She was something else now. Something new.

The air was thick with unspoken words as Tala turned, scanning the faces of her people one last time. The firelight cast long lines across their expressions—some grim, some weary, and others simply resigned. These were the people who had raised her, who had been her family, her blood. But now, they stood apart, watching her go as if she were already a ghost, a spirit slipping away into the unknown.

She searched for understanding in their eyes, some sign that they would not hate her for this. But what she found was quiet resignation, an acceptance laced with sorrow. A few nodded, small gestures of farewell, but many turned away, unwilling or unable to witness her choice. To them, she was no longer Comanche.

Sawáni stood apart from the others, his face unreadable. She had known him since childhood, had grown up racing ponies beside him, learning the ways of the land together. Once, she had thought their lives would always be intertwined, bound by the familiarity of shared youth. But now, that bond was severed. His dark eyes lingered on her, a thousand unspoken words held in their depths, but he said nothing. And then, without a sound, he turned and walked away.

Tala's throat tightened, but she did not call out to him. What was there to say? Goodbye would not change what she had done.

Tsénatokwa stood near the fire, her gaze steady, full of something deeper than disappointment—understanding, perhaps, but also sorrow. The healer did not speak, did not

[CHAPTER 20] — THE COMANCHE BRIDE

try to stop her, for she knew what Tala had come to understand: some paths must be walked alone.

Harrison stood beside her, silent but present, his presence steady. He did not push, did not speak, only waited. She was grateful for that.

Tobáhā finally stepped forward, his expression unreadable. He gave her one last look, a long and measured one, before turning to the warriors at his side. "Let them go," he said, his voice carrying through the camp, firm, absolute.

With that, it was done.

Tala swallowed hard, the weight of finality pressing down on her as she stepped toward the horse that had been prepared for her. She placed a hand on its flank, steadying herself, and then swung up into the saddle. The woven sash from the ceremony still rested against her side, a reminder of the life she had been given, and the one she had chosen instead.

Harrison mounted beside her, the leather cord from their binding ceremony still wrapped around his wrist. It was not lost on her that in some ways, he had been tied to her people just as much as she had been tied to his. But only she was leaving something behind.

Captain Lockwood and his patrol waited, already mounted, their horses restless, their eyes wary. They would not breathe easy until they were back with the regiment.

Harrison leaned over, his gloved hand reaching out, fingers brushing against hers before lacing them together. His grip was firm, solid, offering reassurance even when words failed.

[CHAPTER 20] — THE COMANCHE BRIDE

Tala cast one final glance over her shoulder, back at the village, back at the people who had been her family, her home. The land stretched wide and endless beyond them, the golden grass swaying in the wind, the smoke from the campfires curling toward the sky. She tried to memorize it all—the scent of the earth, the distant calls of the horses, the way the dawn painted the sky in colors that had never felt so bittersweet.

A deep ache filled her chest. This was the only world she had ever known.

And now she was leaving it behind.

She exhaled, tightening her grip on the reins, and turned forward.

With a steady breath, she nudged her horse into motion.

Harrison rode beside her.

The patrol followed.

And together, they left the Comanche camp behind, riding toward a future she could not yet see.

[CHAPTER 21] — A STRANGER IN A NEW LAND

The journey back to Fort Worth stretched long beneath a sky heavy with winter's breath. The land, hardened by cold, bore the weight of hooves and wagon wheels, but it was the silence among the men that carried the heaviest burden. Tension rode thick between the blue-coated soldiers, unspoken judgment coiling in the space between each breath.

Tala rode beside Harrison, her posture rigid, her chin lifted high despite the wary glances cast her way. She would not shrink beneath their eyes, would not let them see weakness—not when she had already given up everything she had ever known. Still, she could feel the weight of their stares, the hushed murmurs that stirred whenever they thought she was not listening.

Some watched her with undisguised suspicion, their hands resting near their weapons as if she might turn on them at any moment. Others stole furtive glances, curiosity warring with unease. She was an outsider in every sense of the word, and she knew, deep down, that no matter how long she rode among them, she would never truly be one of them.

At night, when the fires crackled and the cold bit sharp through the canvas of tents, she kept to herself, sitting just beyond the circle of men as they spoke in low voices. The firelight flickered against their faces, the orange glow unable to soften the lines of distrust etched into their expressions.

"She don't belong here," one of them muttered, his voice barely above the crackle of the flames.

"She's Comanche," another grunted. "She's been living with the same people that ambushed our men last spring."

"She ain't one of them," Harrison's voice cut through the murmurs, sharp as a blade.

The soldiers quieted, but the tension remained, thick in the air. Tala could feel their unease pressing against her like the weight of a storm on the horizon. She kept her gaze on the fire, willing herself not to react, not to let them see that their words stung.

But it wasn't just the whispers—it was the way they looked at Harrison too, the way the trust he had once held among them seemed to have frayed at the edges.

"She turned you against us, Harrison?" a voice challenged from the shadows, and she recognized it as Sergeant Mercer's.

Harrison exhaled sharply, shifting where he sat. "Ain't no one turned me against nothin'. I did what was right."

"What was right?" Mercer scoffed. "You went missing for weeks, and when you show up, you're ridin' in with a Comanche woman at your side like she belongs among us."

Harrison's jaw tightened, his fingers curling around his tin cup as he stared into the flames. "You don't know a damn thing about what happened out there."

"I know enough." Mercer's tone was like gravel. "I know men have died fightin' her people. I know you spent too much time behind enemy lines, and now you're bringin'

[CHAPTER 21] — A STRANGER IN A NEW LAND

one of 'em into our fort. How do we know she ain't just waitin' to slit our throats in the night?"

Tala's grip tightened on her blanket, her breath steady, her pulse loud in her ears. She had expected this. Expected worse. But something about hearing it spoken so plainly sent a cold weight settling in her chest.

Before she could answer, Harrison stood, his boots grinding into the dirt. "You know me, Mercer," he said, his voice even, but there was steel beneath it. "Or at least I thought you did. I ain't askin' you to understand, but you will treat her with respect."

Mercer scoffed but said nothing more. The other soldiers exchanged glances; their expressions unreadable in the dim firelight.

Tala did not speak. Did not move. She only stared into the fire, willing herself to become something unbreakable.

But deep inside, she felt the weight of it—the heavy, inescapable truth.

She had left her people behind.

And she had not yet found a place among these men.

The nights on the trail stretched long, and the soldiers continued to speak of her in hushed tones, thinking her deaf or too ignorant to understand their words. But Tala understood everything. She caught the sneers, the sidelong glances, the muttered insults meant to cut deep.

"Sleeps like a wild dog, probably fights like one too," one man grumbled near the fire, his voice low but not low enough.

[CHAPTER 21] — A STRANGER IN A NEW LAND

Another scoffed. "Ain't nothin' but a savage. He'll see it soon enough."

Tala kept her face impassive, her fingers tightening ever so slightly on the worn edge of her blanket. She had heard worse before, long before she had been forced to make this choice. Their words were sharp, but she had long since learned how to bear the sting.

Harrison, however, had not.

"She understands you," he snapped, his voice cutting through the bitter night air. "Every damn word."

The soldier blinked, clearly caught off guard, but his hesitation lasted only a moment. "That so?" he mused, his mouth twitching into something that was not quite a smile. "Well, maybe she oughta hear it, then."

Harrison took a step forward, but before his fist could find a target, Tala's hand landed lightly on his forearm. He turned, meeting her steady gaze. She shook her head once, firm but calm.

She would not let this be her first fight among them.

Harrison hesitated; his jaw clenched so tightly she could see the muscle twitch. Slowly, his fingers uncurled, but his fury did not fade. He turned back to the fire, his glare promising that this was not over.

The men quieted after that, but only for a time. The whispers always returned, crawling through the camp like embers waiting to set dry brush aflame.

One evening, as they sat apart from the others, sharing a meal beneath the vast, open sky, the murmurs turned crueler.

[CHAPTER 21] — A STRANGER IN A NEW LAND

"A Comanche bride?" one soldier muttered. "He's lost his damn mind."

Harrison's grip on his tin cup tightened until his knuckles turned white. His breath came hard and fast, like a horse ready to charge into a fight. Tala, who had already known this moment would come, reached for his arm again. This time, she pressed her fingers lightly against his sleeve, her touch enough to still him.

"They are just words," she murmured.

He exhaled sharply through his nose, his anger slow to settle. "They ain't right."

Tala met his gaze, her expression unreadable. "That does not matter."

Harrison let out a frustrated breath, shaking his head. "It does to me."

She gave him a look then—one he was beginning to learn, one that spoke of all the things she would not say aloud.

"I have endured worse than whispers," she said quietly. "I will not break now."

For a moment, neither spoke.

Then, reluctantly, Harrison nodded, the tension in his body easing ever so slightly. But Tala knew better. He would not forget. He would not let this go so easily.

And neither, she suspected, would the men around them.

Several days later, the fort loomed on the horizon, a stark and unyielding shape against the dying light of the sky. Its walls, built of rough-hewn logs and packed earth, were

[CHAPTER 21] — A STRANGER IN A NEW LAND

nothing like the open plains Tala had once called home. There was no wind moving freely through the grass, no sky stretching endlessly above. Here, the air was thick with the scent of smoke and sweat, with the sound of boots striking hard-packed ground. It felt closed, trapped—a place made for men who feared the wilderness beyond its walls.

As they rode through the open gates, a hush fell over the yard. Soldiers turned, their conversations fading mid-sentence. Settlers paused in their work, eyes narrowing as they took in the sight of Tala riding among them. Mothers gripped their children's arms, pulling them closer, as if her very presence was a threat. Some of the men muttered, their gazes dark with suspicion. The weight of their stares pressed against her, thick as a winter storm rolling in.

Harrison rode beside her, his jaw set tight, his fingers flexing around the reins as he took in the reception. He had known it would be like this—had prepared himself for it—but seeing it unfold made his blood burn.

One soldier sneered under his breath. "Hell's he think he's doin', bringin' her here?"

"Best keep your scalp covered," another muttered.

Tala caught the words but did not react. She had learned long ago how to hold herself still, how to keep her expression unreadable when the world turned against her. But she felt Harrison shift beside her, his shoulders tensing, his breath coming a little sharper.

She turned slightly toward him, barely tilting her chin. *Do not fight.* The unspoken command passed between them in the space of a heartbeat.

[CHAPTER 21] — A STRANGER IN A NEW LAND

The murmurs grew, rippling through the gathered men like dry brush catching fire. But before the embers could blaze, the doors to the command post swung open.

Major Ripley A. Arnold stepped forward, his blue officer's coat crisp against the dust of the fort. He was a tall man, broad-shouldered, with an expression carved from stone. His sharp eyes swept across the gathered men before settling on Tala. He looked her over, slow and deliberate, his mouth pressing into a thin line.

Then he turned to Captain Lockwood.

"This is no place for an Indian," Arnold said, his voice flat, carrying easily over the murmuring crowd.

The weight of the words settled over the yard, thick as a storm cloud ready to break.

Harrison straightened in the saddle. "She's with me."

Arnold's gaze flicked to him, unimpressed. "So I gathered." His tone was edged with something unreadable, something that carried a warning. "And I assume there's an explanation for why you rode into my fort with a Comanche woman at your side?"

Harrison's knuckles whitened against the reins. "I brought her because she had nowhere else to go."

Arnold let the words hang in the air, his expression unreadable. Then he turned, leveling his gaze at Tala once more.

She met it without flinching.

His lips pressed together, and when he spoke again, there was no warmth in his voice. "You're under my command now, Sergeant. You should've known better."

Tala felt Harrison's breath hitch—just barely—but before he could speak, Lockwood cut in.

"She's here under my authority, sir," Lockwood said. "She's not a prisoner. We negotiated a truce with her people before we left."

Arnold raised a brow. "A truce?"

"Yes," Lockwood confirmed. "For the winter."

The major let out a slow, measured breath, as if deciding how much patience he had left. "And you expect me to believe that?"

Lockwood's face remained impassive. "It's the truth."

Arnold's eyes narrowed, his gaze shifting between them, searching for cracks. Then he exhaled sharply, shaking his head.

"I'll discuss this in my office," he said at last. "And you'd best have something worth saying." His cold gaze landed on Tala one last time before he turned. "As for her—she stays out of the way. I won't have her stirring up trouble."

With that, he strode back toward the command post.

The crowd lingered a moment longer, eyes still heavy on Tala, before slowly dissipating. But the tension in the air did not fade.

Harrison let out a slow breath, his fingers still tight around the reins. "Well," he muttered, voice dry, "that went about how I expected."

Tala said nothing. She only stared at the doors where the major had disappeared, knowing the worst had yet to come.

[CHAPTER 22] — THE COST OF LOVE

The fort was a world of stiff backs and rigid stares, its walls looming high, not just in stone but in the unspoken divide that kept her apart from those who called it home. Tala moved through the days in silence, her presence tolerated but never accepted. She knew the looks they cast her way—the narrowed gazes of soldiers, the wary glances of their wives, the way the women whispered behind their hands when they thought she could not hear. They saw her as something foreign, something wild, a piece of the plains that did not belong within these walls.

She did not need to understand all their words to know what they said. Some of the soldiers ignored her outright, treating her as if she were no more than a passing wind, something unseen and unimportant. Others watched her openly, suspicion flickering in their eyes, their hands drifting to their rifles when she passed too close. The women in the fort, wives of officers and settlers, were worse in their way. Their stares burned colder; their words dipped in quiet venom.

"She does not belong here," one woman murmured to another as Tala walked past. "Bringing one of them into the fort... what was that man thinking?"

Tala did not slow her steps, did not turn to acknowledge them. She had endured worse. She had been judged by both sides for what she was, neither Comanche nor white. The words of these women could not wound her, but still, they settled heavy in her chest.

[CHAPTER 22] — THE COST OF LOVE

Even those closest to Harrison did not know what to make of her. The men who had served beside him, who had once fought at his side without question, now watched him with doubt. Their loyalty to him clashed with the prejudices they had been raised with. They did not trust her, and because of that, they no longer trusted him. Harrison did not speak of it, but she could see it in his jaw when he clenched his teeth, in the way his shoulders tensed when he walked through the barracks.

She could not change their hearts, nor did she try. Instead, she turned to what she knew—healing. If they would not see her as one of them, then she would remind them that she was not their enemy.

She sought out the sick and the injured, offering her skills where she could. The fort's doctor, an older man with more lines of worry than wisdom, scoffed at her presence at first. "What could you possibly know of medicine?" he asked, his eyes sharp as he looked her over.

Tala met his gaze without flinching. "More than you, when it comes to these lands."

At first, he refused her, waving her away like a nuisance. But the soldiers had wounds that festered, fevers that burned hot, and when the remedies the doctor had did not work, it was Tala they came to in the quiet hours of the night. She did not turn them away. She ground herbs into pastes, pressed cool cloths against burning skin, bound wounds with steady hands. She did what she had always done—she healed.

There were those who accepted her aid begrudgingly, and others who still turned their noses up at her, choosing

[CHAPTER 22] — THE COST OF LOVE

pain over pride. But there were also those who began to look at her with something other than distrust. A young private, no older than sixteen, who had taken an arrow to the arm and watched in amazement as the swelling went down under her treatment. A grizzled soldier who had seen too many battles, who nodded at her one morning as she passed, a silent acknowledgment of the pain she had eased.

And yet, for every man she healed, there were ten more who would never accept her, no matter what she did.

One night, as she walked past a group of soldiers gathered near the barracks, their voices low and laughing, she caught the words as they drifted through the cool air.

"Sergeant Harrison's got himself a Comanche wife now," one of them muttered. "Lost his damn mind, if you ask me."

Another chuckled. "Maybe he just likes things to be a little wild in his bed."

The laughter rippled through the group, crude and knowing, and something in Tala twisted. But before she could step away, before she could make the choice to ignore them, Harrison was there. His hand curled into a fist at his side, his jaw tight.

"What did you say?" His voice was low, steady, but there was a sharpness to it, a blade's edge beneath the calm.

The men turned, amusement flickering in their eyes. "Just talking, Sergeant," one said, lifting his hands as if in innocence. "Didn't mean nothing by it."

"Didn't mean nothing by it," Harrison repeated, his voice quiet but dangerous. He stepped forward, his

[CHAPTER 22] — THE COST OF LOVE

shoulders squared, and the men tensed. "Then say it again. Say it now, to my face."

The laughter faded. No one spoke.

Tala placed a hand on his arm, shaking her head. "Let it be," she murmured.

His muscles were tight beneath her fingers, his fury barely contained. But after a moment, he exhaled, turning from the men, walking away. She followed, feeling the weight of their eyes on her back.

When they were far enough away, she finally spoke. "I have heard worse."

"That doesn't make it right." His voice was still rough, still filled with the anger he had not been able to unleash.

"No," she agreed. "But you cannot fight every battle with your fists."

He turned to her then, his blue eyes dark. "And what about you?" he asked. "How long do I let you fight this battle alone?"

Tala did not have an answer. Because no matter how many wounds she mended, she could not heal the rift that existed between her and the world she had stepped into.

The tension in the fort had become a living thing, thick and unrelenting. Harrison fought for her, just as she knew he would, challenging the stares, the whispers, and the outright insults that surfaced when men forgot—or simply no longer cared—that she could understand them. But no matter how many times he stood between her and their contempt, no matter how fiercely he defended her, he could not change the way these men had been raised to see her.

[CHAPTER 22] — THE COST OF LOVE

One afternoon, Harrison came back from a meeting with his superiors, his shoulders stiff, his jaw set like iron. He did not speak right away, just strode past her toward their quarters, each step heavy with something unspoken. Tala felt it settle between them, pressing against her like the weight of an oncoming storm.

She waited for him to speak, but when the silence stretched too long, she finally stepped closer. "What happened?" she asked.

Harrison exhaled through his nose, rubbing a hand across his face before meeting her gaze. "Nothing I didn't expect." His tone was even, too even, but she could see the anger beneath it, the barely contained fury simmering just beneath his skin.

"Tell me," she pressed.

He hesitated, then sighed. "Major Arnold isn't pleased," he admitted. "Made it clear I have a choice to make."

Tala did not ask what choice. She already knew.

That night, long after the fires had burned low, she heard the voices carrying across the fort. She was returning from the infirmary, where she had spent the evening tending to a young soldier with an infected wound, when the sound of Major Arnold's voice drifted through the cool night air. She paused, just beyond the reach of the torchlight, unseen but listening.

"You're a fine soldier, Sergeant Harrison," Arnold was saying, his voice clipped, carrying the authority of a man

[CHAPTER 22] — THE COST OF LOVE

who was not used to being questioned. "One of the best I've got. I don't want to see your career wasted."

There was a pause, then the sound of boots shifting in the dirt.

"But?" Harrison's voice was quiet, steady, though Tala could hear the steel beneath it.

Arnold did not hesitate. "But a soldier's loyalty belongs to his country, not to some Comanche woman."

Tala felt her breath catch, the words hitting sharper than any blade. She had known this moment would come; had known from the moment she had ridden through those gates at Harrison's side that there would be no easy road ahead. But hearing it spoken aloud, hearing the cold finality in the Major's tone, made it real in a way it had not been before.

Harrison's response came swift and firm. "She is my wife. That is not changing."

His voice did not waver, did not soften. It rang with conviction, with defiance, and for a moment, Tala's heart lifted.

But then she saw him turn away, she caught the tightness in his shoulders, the battle weighing down on him. He had drawn a line in the dirt, but the cost of standing by her was becoming clearer with each passing day.

She remained where she was, unseen in the dark, her chest tight with the weight of the truth she had always known but had never wanted to face.

Some battles could not be won.

The night air carried a chill, but Tala hardly felt it. She sat at the edge of the fort, just beyond the glow of the

[CHAPTER 22] — THE COST OF LOVE

watchfires, staring out at the endless plains beyond the wooden walls. The land stretched far, quiet and untouched, but it was no longer hers. The realization settled in her chest like a stone.

She had made her choice, but at what cost?

Was she selfish for staying? Was it wrong to ask Harrison to give up everything for her when she knew what it would mean for him? His place among his people, his uniform, his purpose—all of it now slipping through his fingers because of her. Because he had chosen her.

A soft rustling of footsteps broke her thoughts, and she didn't need to turn to know who it was. Harrison always moved with a certain weight, a presence that filled the space around him without demanding it. He stopped just behind her, silent for a long moment, as if waiting to see if she would send him away. When she didn't, he sat beside her, stretching his long legs in front of him, resting his elbows on his knees.

"They will never accept me," she murmured finally, staring down at her hands.

He didn't answer right away. Instead, he reached over, his fingers brushing against hers before lacing them together, strong and sure. He gave her hand a squeeze. "Then we'll make our own place."

She let out a quiet breath, shaking her head. "And where is that? There is no place in this world where we belong."

"I used to think the same," he admitted. His voice was low, rough around the edges, like a man who had carried too

[CHAPTER 22] — THE COST OF LOVE

much weight for too long. "For a long time, I didn't belong anywhere. I left home and wandered for so long. Then I fought in a war I barely understood, and now I have signed up to fight another war. But after all that, you know what I realized?"

She turned to look at him then, her dark eyes searching his face.

"I don't want to fight anymore," he said, his voice quiet but firm. "Not against your people. Not against anyone. I thought wearing this uniform meant something, but now I see it for what it is. A war that never ends. A fight that never should've started." His grip on her hand tightened. "I don't need this fort, or this army. The only thing I need is you."

Tala's throat tightened. She had braced herself for his doubt, for regret, for hesitation. But not this. Not a vow spoken so simply, so freely, as if he had no fear of what it would cost him.

"You would give it all up?" she asked, her voice barely above a whisper.

He nodded, the firelight catching in his blue eyes, turning them to steel. "I think I already have."

She held his gaze, searching for any flicker of uncertainty. There was none. He had made his choice, and it was her. And yet, even as warmth bloomed in her chest, she could not quiet the doubt creeping into her mind.

Love was fierce, but was it enough to withstand the weight of the world pressing against them? She had no answer, only the feel of his hand in hers and the knowledge that, for now, he had chosen her.

[CHAPTER 23] — A FIRE THAT WILL NEVER DIE

The following night, as the sun dipped below the horizon, the sky burned with streaks of crimson and deep indigo. The dying light stretched across the plains, setting the land ablaze in a final display before night swallowed it whole. Tala stood outside the fort, her arms wrapped around herself, though the chill in the air was nothing compared to the ache in her chest.

She had never been meant for walls. The open plains had always been her home, where the wind carried the scent of rain and wild grass, where she had been free to move beneath the endless sky. Now, all she could smell was the dust kicked up by soldiers' boots and the smoke curling from the chimneys of a place that was not hers. The wind stirred her hair, tangling it around her face, as if trying to pull her back to what she had left behind.

She did not hear Harrison approach, but she felt him before he spoke, his presence as familiar as the earth beneath her feet.

"If you wish to leave," he said, his voice low, steady, "I will not stop you."

Tala turned slowly, her dark eyes locking onto his. He stood just a few feet away, his features unreadable in the dimming light, but his meaning was clear. She searched his face, expecting to find fear or hesitation, perhaps even

[CHAPTER 23] — A FIRE THAT WILL NEVER DIE

doubt. But there was none. Only love—pure, unwavering love. Not chains, not possession, not desperation. Just love.

Her throat tightened. "Do you want me to go?"

Harrison exhaled through his nose, shaking his head. "No." He took a step closer, his voice softer now. "I would fight for you, Tala. I am happy to give up everything I have left to be with you." His jaw tensed as he looked past her toward the plains, where the last of the sun's light touched the land she once called home. "But I won't force you to stay where you are not wanted."

She understood what he meant. The fort was a cage, and the people within it had made no secret of their disdain for her. But she had known that would be the case before she ever set foot inside these walls. She had made her choice with open eyes. And now, as she looked at the man who had risked everything for her, she knew she would make it again.

She stepped forward, reaching for his hand. He stilled as her fingers laced through his, warm against the cool night air.

"I did not leave my people to run," she whispered. "I will fight for this, too."

A slow breath left Harrison's lips, as if he had been holding it in. He squeezed her hand, his grip firm and sure, and in that moment, she knew they would stand together—against the world if they had to.

The night stretched long and quiet, the sky a vast canvas of silver pinpricks burning through the darkness. A breath of wind stirred the dry grass around them, carrying the scent of earth and distant rain, as if the land itself

[CHAPTER 23] — A FIRE THAT WILL NEVER DIE

whispered of what had come before and what was yet to come. Tala lay beside Harrison, her body pressed against the solid warmth of his, her head resting lightly on his chest. The steady rhythm of his heartbeat beneath her ear anchored her in the moment, even as the world outside these plains sought to pull them apart.

She stared up at the endless sprawl of stars, tracing familiar constellations the way she had as a child. She wondered how many of her ancestors had looked upon this same sky, whispered the same prayers, carried the same ache in their hearts for something just beyond reach. And now, she was here, lying in the arms of a man who was not of her people, yet who had become hers in ways she had never expected.

She spoke softly in Comanche, letting the words slip between them like water over smooth stones. "Tupunakatu," she murmured, her voice no louder than the rustle of the grass. "Strength."

Harrison's lips curved faintly as he repeated it, his voice careful, reverent. "Tupunakatu."

She shifted slightly, tilting her head to look at him in the dim glow of the moon. "Tsaatu."

He hesitated, his brow furrowing slightly as he worked through the shape of the word. "Tsaatu," he said at last, the syllables still foreign on his tongue.

"Love," she translated, watching his reaction.

Harrison was quiet for a long moment, then rolled onto his side, his hand finding hers between them. He traced a thumb over her knuckles, his blue eyes dark with something deep and unshakable. "Tsaatu," he said again, firmer this time, as if committing it not just to memory, but to his very bones.

Tala smiled, warmth spreading through her chest, pressing against her ribs as if it had nowhere else to go. She leaned in, pressing a kiss to his temple, feeling the slight hitch in his breath as her lips brushed his skin. "You are my home now," she whispered.

Harrison exhaled, his grip tightening on her hand as if afraid she might slip through his fingers. "Then we leave tomorrow," he murmured, his voice a quiet promise.

She nodded, her heart steady with the certainty of it. The fort would never welcome her, the soldiers would never accept her, but she had already chosen her path. She would not be erased. She would not bow beneath the weight of their judgment.

As the wind curled through the night, she closed her eyes and listened. It carried the voices of those who had come before, their strength woven into the fabric of the land. She could feel them, could hear them in the rustling grass, in the distant cry of the night hawk, in the breath of the man beside her.

Their story was only beginning.

And they would write it in a fire that would never die, in love that would never die, and in a strength that would never yield.

ABOUT THE AUTHOR

Samuel DenHartog is a passionate storyteller with a deep love for capturing the rugged beauty and untamed spirit of the American frontier. His historical romances weave together vivid landscapes, compelling characters, and the indomitable human will, bringing the Wild West to life in every tale. Samuel's dedication to detail and his ability to immerse readers in a bygone era make his stories not only captivating but also a heartfelt homage to the resilience and passion that defined the Old West.

Drawing inspiration from the strength and determination of pioneers, ranchers, and dreamers who shaped the frontier, Samuel creates rich narratives filled with romance, adventure, and the enduring power of hope. Each of his characters reflects the struggles and triumphs of a time when love was as wild and unpredictable as the untamed land itself. With a keen eye for historical accuracy and a talent for crafting unforgettable relationships, Samuel's works resonate deeply with readers seeking stories of courage and connection.

When not crafting his latest book, Samuel enjoys exploring the history and culture of the world, finding inspiration in the tales of those who came before. His passion for storytelling is matched by his commitment to honoring the spirit of resilience, love, and adventure that defines the heart of his novels. Through his writing, Samuel invites readers to embark on journeys filled with grit, determination, and the timeless pursuit of love.

Made in the USA
Middletown, DE
03 April 2025

73746135R00125